COMING HOME TO HONEY GROVE

A BRAXTON FAMILY ROMANCE BOOK 1

ANNE-MARIE MEYER

To my PA and Friend, Trisha
Thanks for taking this crazy journey with me

ONE

JOSH

JOSH BRAXTON PULLED into the driveway of his childhood home and turned off the engine of his truck. Humiliation, frustration, and pain clung to his chest like a cold he couldn't kick as he stared at the familiar two-story house with red shutters and a porch that wrapped all the way around the first floor.

This was his new life. Everything he'd ever done had led up to this moment.

Seriously?

Leaving this house at eighteen only to be back here fourteen years later hadn't been his dream. But neither had being left by his now ex-wife.

It's funny how your life can change its course without first consulting you.

"Are we here?" Jordan asked from the back seat.

Josh winced at his five-year-old's idea of an inside voice.

"Headphones, JP," Josh said, turning and pointing to his ears.

Jordan pulled his headphones off and glanced around. His nose wrinkled. "This is where we are living?"

Josh swallowed and took in a deep breath. Even his son knew how pathetic it was that he had to move back in with his parents.

"Yep. Aren't you excited to stay with Nana and Papa?" Josh forced a smile.

Jordan shrugged. "They have good cookies."

Josh snorted. That was true. His mother had won her share of blue first-place ribbons for her baking here in Honey Grove, SC. Which was a good thing. With five boys to feed, she'd needed to cook. A lot.

Josh pulled open his door and stepped out, stretching in the warm sun. He loved South Carolina in the summer. It reminded him of popsicles and trips to the beach. And, if he were honest, he was ready to share this life with his son.

Jordan slammed the door as he got out of the car. "It's hot," he said, squinting up at Josh.

"Get used to it, buddy. It won't cool down for another few months."

This was definitely different than the picturesque Colorado home he'd given up in the divorce. Josh's ex-wife, Cindy, had decided that she wanted nothing to do with either of them and had moved her new husband into their mountain home.

Those were her terms for giving him sole custody. She'd

given up her son and husband for his twenty-five-year-old partner. Man, he was such an idiot.

Heat pricked at the back of Josh's neck, and it wasn't from the weather. It was a feeling he got every time he thought about Cindy. How could any mother just give up on her son like that?

Staring down at Jordan's shaggy hair and big, missing-his-front-teeth grin, Josh knew there was nothing in the world that would keep him away from his son.

Nothing.

"My baby's home!" Sondra Braxton shouted from the front porch. Her greying black hair was pulled up into a messy bun and dark-red glasses perched on her nose. She was rounder than he remembered. Her flour-covered apron, wrapped around her five-foot-four frame, strained against her stomach.

"Hey, Ma," Josh said as he slammed his door and walked across the grass.

He had to dip down to wrap his arms around her. He was six-foot-two, the tallest of the five Braxton boys. His mom wrapped her arms around his shoulders and gave him one of her signature *I'm going to squeeze you like a snake* hugs.

"I'm so happy you're here," she said, pulling back and wiping away a tear.

"Woman, stop your blubbering," Jimmy Braxton said with a grin.

Josh smiled up at his dad, who'd appeared from around

the house. He was wiping his hands on a rag as he approached.

"Jordan!" Sondra rushed to go smother her grandson with hugs and kisses.

Josh and his dad shook hands for a moment before embracing. After their quick hug, Jimmy pulled back.

"Everything is set for you. The guys are excited to have a Braxton boy working with them again."

Josh pushed his hands through his curly brown hair and nodded. After the divorce, he'd decided to take a sabbatical from practicing law. The man his wife had left him for was his business partner, and, right now, his heart just wasn't in the work that used to consume him from sunup to sundown.

"Great. Can't wait to start," Josh said, hoping his fake enthusiasm was good enough to fool his father.

Jimmy paused and squinted over at Josh. Josh could see that his dad wanted to ask another question.

"Just spit it out, Dad."

Jimmy cleared his throat and shifted his weight from one foot to the other. "Are you sure this is what you want? I mean, you've always been more into the books. Are you going to be satisfied in construction?"

Josh flexed his muscles. He had the itch to move—his pent up frustration didn't go well with sitting behind a desk. "Physical labor might be just what I need."

Jimmy nodded. "Okay. Well, you know you can leave anytime you want. I mean, you're not obligated to stay.

Whenever you're ready to go back to lawyering, I won't be hurt."

Josh reached out and clapped his hand on his dad's shoulder. "I appreciate that."

"Stop trying to push my son out of my house. I just got him back," Sondra said, walking up to them.

Jimmy raised his hands. "I warned you. Once you're back in her nest, this momma bird isn't going to let you go that easily."

Josh laughed. "Heard you loud and clear."

"I've got to pee," Jordan announced, so Jimmy excused himself to show Jordan to the bathroom.

Josh turned his attention to his mom. She was smiling up at him.

"What?" he asked, moving back across the lawn to his truck. He pulled the tailgate open and started unloading boxes.

"I'm just glad you're home, that's all. It's been too quiet since y'all left."

Josh nodded. Growing up with five siblings made every day pretty eventful—never a dull moment. But they were all grown up now and were doing different things. At least, everyone else was. Josh was coming home. Starting back at the beginning.

But his mom looked so happy that he was home, he didn't want to crush her spirits. So he gave her a smile as he pulled a box labeled *Jordan's Toys* out of the back.

"Have you heard from any of them?" he asked, wanting

to take the attention off himself. He was pretty close to cracking, but breaking down in front of his mom was the last thing he should do if he wanted to maintain his sanity.

Sondra sighed as she leaned against the truck. "Well, Jonathan is still in Pittsburgh. I think he's planning on coming home before the season starts up again. James is as elusive as ever. I thought getting out of the military would finally bring him home." She grew quiet and Josh looked over to see the sadness in her eyes.

"Ma, you know James. That's just his personality. We could never tie him down."

Sondra patted her cheeks. "I know, I know. I just worry about him."

Josh nodded. That was something he hadn't understood until he had a son of his own. The constant worry of a parent.

"I talked to Jackson last week. He's buying an apartment in New York." Sondra continued.

Jackson Braxton—also known as the rich Braxton brother. Josh smiled. "Why am I not surprised?"

Sondra chuckled. "And Dean is here. He's coming for dinner tonight. The charity he set up in his mom's name has really taken off. It's keeping him busy."

Dean Diego, the foster boy his parents took in to finish his senior year in Honey Grove. Even though he wasn't blood, he was still a Braxton and a brother.

"What about Jenna?" Josh asked, his chest swelled with

concern for his little sister. She was the youngest Braxton and the only girl.

Sondra's lips tipped up into a smile. "She's doing well. Finishing her internship in Seattle. I think she's planning on coming back if the county doesn't give her a job."

Josh lowered the last box to the ground. He missed his little sister. Even though they were eight years apart, he'd always taken it upon himself to protect her and look out for her.

A yellow bug drove by and slowed as it pulled into the Johnson's driveway across the street. Intrigued with who was driving, Josh straightened and squinted. The parking lights turned off and the driver door opened.

"Oh, and I didn't tell you. Beth is back."

Josh's ears pricked at the name of the girl who'd grown up across the street. The one who had once proclaimed her love to him. He chuckled.

"Beth's back?" Last he'd heard, she was dating some business man and had moved to Philadelphia.

Sondra nodded. "And single."

Josh shot his mom an exasperated look. "I'm not—why does that matter?"

Sondra shrugged and they both turned to see Beth step out of her car.

Josh's heart picked up speed as she flicked her long, blonde hair off her shoulder and shouldered her purse. She was wearing a pair of cutoffs, and Josh was trying really hard not to notice how long and tan her legs had gotten. Or the fact that her white tank was filled out quite nicely.

She was definitely not the short, thin girl he remembered.

"Beth," Sondra yelled, raising her hand.

"Ma," Josh said under his breath. This was the last thing he needed—his mom meddling in his love life.

Startled, Beth glanced up, and Josh thought that he saw her cheeks redden when her gaze fell on him. But, when he blinked, she looked much more relaxed.

Josh gave her a small wave and he cursed himself for thinking she'd had any reaction to him. It must have been his imagination. But then he felt even more like an idiot. Why was Beth blushing something he would imagine? Why did he care?

He was rusty at this whole needing to interpret what women were thinking bit. It'd been years since he even needed to think about flirting. And if his past experience with love was any indication of his future, he should just throw in the towel now. Love wasn't worth that kind of pain.

"Hey, Mrs. B," Beth said, raising her hand and waving. "Josh."

"Come over here, sweetheart. Look who's come back home."

Josh shot his mom an annoyed look, but if she noticed, she didn't care.

Beth glanced down at her watch and then back up at them. "I'm—I should really—"

"Nonsense. I'm sure whatever you have going on isn't as important as greeting an old friend."

Josh parted his lips to come to Beth's rescue, but closed his mouth when he saw her nod and make her way toward them. After crossing the street, she walked up, pausing a few feet away.

"Did you know that Josh is back to stay?" his mom asked, peering up at Beth.

Beth turned her gaze up to Josh and nodded. Her blue eyes were as bright as ever, but there was something about them. Age had made her more beautiful than he remembered. Or, perhaps, it was the light dusting of freckles across her nose or her full, red lips...

"Josh, say hi to Beth."

Realizing that he was just standing there, staring, Josh took a deep breath and extended his hand. He needed to get a grip. "Right." He gave her a smile. "Hi, Beth."

She chuckled, and the sound of her laugh did strange things to his insides. "Hi, Josh." She pinched her lips together as she glanced up at him. "It's nice to have you back."

He wasn't sure if she meant it or if that was something she said to everyone, but from the way his stomach lightened, he couldn't help but hope that she meant it.

"It's good to be back," he said. For the first time in a long time, hope grew in his chest. Being home might not be so bad after all.

When he realized that he was still holding her hand, he

dropped it and gave her an apologetic smile. Her lips were tipped up at the corners as she glanced at Sondra.

"I should really get going," Beth said apologetically.

Sondra nodded. "Of course. You promise you'll come over for our celebratory dinner?"

Beth's lips parted, and she looked as if she were searching for a polite way to reject his mom's offer.

"Ma, she probably has plans," Josh said, giving her a sympathetic smile.

"Nonsense. She has nothing to do that's more important than my pot roast. Come. It will be fun to catch up. You two have lots to talk about, I'm sure," Sondra said, wiggling her eyebrows.

Beth studied her for a moment, her eyebrows knit together. "I'll try to come." Then her gaze rose to meet his. There was a shy hint to her expression. "It might be nice to catch up."

Josh swallowed from the unexpected heat that flushed his skin. Instead, he tried to focus on his mom as she told Beth the time and extended the invitation to her parents as well.

Beth thanked her, shot one last look at Josh, and headed back across the street.

Turning, Josh glared at his mom. "What was that?" he asked as he heaved a box up onto his shoulder and headed for the apartment over the garage. The Braxton Hotel, his mom called it.

Sondra shrugged. "I'm sure I don't know what you

mean."

Josh turned the handle and stepped inside. "What are you trying to do? Why were you so insistent that Beth come for dinner?"

Sondra opened her mouth in mock surprise as she held her hand to her chest. "I'm choosing to ignore the fact that you think I had ulterior motives. There is nothing devious about asking an old friend to dinner."

Josh chuckled. "Right." He stuck his finger out at his mom. "You've never tried to play matchmaker for your sons?"

Sondra's face contorted as she tried to keep a straight face. "I don't know what you are talking about."

Josh watched his mom and then sighed. "Just don't go crazy, Ma. I'm not ready for any of that yet. Or maybe ever."

Sondra's expression grew serious as she crossed the room and gave him a hug. "I know, honey. I wouldn't dream of pushing you when you're not ready. It wouldn't be fair to you or the girl."

Josh wrapped one arm around his mom and nodded as he rested his chin on her head. "Thanks."

She gave him one last squeeze and then hurried toward the door. "My cookies," she said in a panic. Right before she disappeared down the stairs, she turned. "I'm really glad you're home."

Josh straightened and looked around at the familiar, dated furniture. She was right. For now, this was his home, and he was glad to be back. "Me too."

TWO

BETH

BETH HURRIED across the street and into her parent's house. Once the door was shut, she leaned against it and closed her eyes, her heart pounding.

Why did fate have such a cruel sense of humor? Why did it bring Josh Braxton back into her life right when she was pretty sure she couldn't go any lower?

She was jobless, relationship-less, and, right now, directionless.

This was not the time to bring back the guy she'd crushed on during all of her teenage years.

It didn't help that Josh got even more good-looking than she remembered. He'd grown from a tall, lanky teenage boy to a full-blown man. The memory of his five o'clock shadow and half-smile caused her stomach to lighten and her pulse to quicken—just as it did fifteen years ago.

And when he'd moved to shake her hand, she about had

a heart attack there in the Braxtons' driveway. Especially when his black t-shirt did nothing to hide the muscles under his sleeves.

She reached up and fanned her face as a blush started on her cheeks and rushed across her whole body. Man. She was in major trouble.

"Oh, you're back." Her mom, Joanne, said as she rounded the corner. She was still in her pajamas—something she was doing more and more lately.

Beth pushed off the door and gave her mom a weary smile. "Hey, Mom." She ran her gaze over Joanne and worry brewed in her gut. "How are you feeling today?"

Joanne let out an exasperated sigh. "Can we not do that? I don't have the energy."

Beth bit her lip, trying to push down the pain that crept up in her gut every time she thought of her mother's diagnosis. Cancer. It didn't help that it was compounded with the strained relationship they'd had since her parents divorced when Beth was a teenager. But, for right now, the past could just be the past. She needed to focus on the reason she was here. Why she'd decided to stay, even though their relationship was fractured to the point of breaking.

Beth only just found out about the cancer a couple of weeks ago. Her mom had decided to keep it a secret from her. Apparently it wasn't important enough to tell her daughter about. She'd played it off like she didn't want to put added stress on Beth, but Beth knew better. And when

Beth's boyfriend, Zander, dumped her, she thought coming home for a visit would be a good idea.

It wasn't until she was living under the same roof as her mom and step-dad that the truth came out. Now, Beth was stuck. When she found out how much they were floundering financially, the feeling of responsibility weighed on her. With the illness, Beth was trying to put the past behind her and build a relationship with her mom no matter what.

If only she could find a job, maybe her mom wouldn't think her stay was worthless. But it seemed as if no one in Honey Grove was hiring. If someone had told her that a Psychology degree wouldn't lead to a job, perhaps, she would have picked a different career field. And maybe graduate college with a little less debt.

Joanne shuffled over to the TV and collapsed onto the recliner. Beth swallowed when she saw the balding spot on the back of her mom's head. A cruel reminder of the disease.

"Water?" Beth asked, moving toward the kitchen. She needed a job. She couldn't just stand here and stare at her frail mom.

Joanne muttered something under her breath, and Beth took it as affirmation and filled up a glass. After slipping a few ice cubes and a straw into it, she set the cup down on the end table next to the recliner.

Her mom reached out and grabbed her hand before she could leave. "Did you find a job?" she asked, giving Beth a critical look.

Beth's heart squeezed as she shook her head. "No, not yet. But I'm not giving up."

Her mom shifted on the seat, closing her eyes as pain radiated across her face. "You shouldn't be here. This isn't your life," she whispered as she tipped her head up, resting it on the back of the chair.

It hurt that her mom could be so cruel. Beth took a deep breath. She could handle this. If her mother wasn't sick, things would look different. Besides, she couldn't turn her back on her mom. Not when she was sick. Even if it felt as if her mother didn't trust her with anything.

"It's okay, I'm here. You shouldn't go through this alone."

Her mom opened her eyes and studied Beth. "I just can't handle the stress of taking care of you, too," she whispered. Beth could see frustration simmering in her mom's gaze.

Beth knelt down as she tried to swallow the pain that clung to her throat. "I won't be a burden. I promise, I will help. We'll get through this."

Joanne studied her for a moment before she covered their grasped hands with her other one. "I know. I just hurt so much." She gave Beth a small smile as the pain raced across her face. "I'm sorry to be so short with you. It's hard having you around, reminding me of all the things you are giving up. The life you should be living."

All Beth could do was nod. There were moments with her mom that hurt, but then there were moments like this when the mom she remembered from before the divorce came shining through. It was that side of her mom that made Beth want to be here.

But the fact that her mom thought she even had a life was laughable. Guys and employers weren't exactly lining up for a broke, jobless, twenty-eight-year-old.

Her mom's smile faltered as she motioned for the remote. Beth handed it over and then straightened, making her way over to the stairs.

Then she remembered Mrs. Braxton and the commitment she'd made for dinner tonight, so she turned, pausing in the doorway. "Hey, Mom?"

Joanne gave a small moan in response.

"Mrs. Braxton invited us over for dinner tonight." She hesitated, waiting for her mom's reaction.

Just as her mom and stepdad had kept her mom's illness from her, they were also keeping it from everyone they knew. They said it was to keep her mom strong. That pity looks were the last thing they needed—but Beth was sure there was something more.

Telling people about the disease would give it life. Acknowledging she had cancer meant acknowledging the fact that she might not make it. That she could become just another statistic.

Beth hated secrets and lies, but it wasn't her truth to tell, and she respected her mom enough to keep it a secret.

For now.

"We're not going," her mom said.

Beth nodded. That's what she'd figured.

"But you should go. We don't want people to suspect. Just tell Sondra that I'm tired."

Beth rubbed her temples as she muttered a quick, "Okay," and then headed to her room. Once inside, she flopped down on her bed and sighed into her comforter.

The stress of her situation bore down on her, and she felt she just might break. It wasn't anywhere near the dream life she used to entertain as a kid.

Rolling to her back, she stared up at the ceiling. The memory of Josh standing in front of her floated through her mind.

Her phone rang. She jumped and reached into her back pocket.

It was Tiffany. Her best friend since elementary school.

Sighing, she brought the phone to her cheek. "Hello?"

"Beth?"

"Hey, Tiff."

"I can't believe you're back! I get home from Paris to find out my best friend came home? What are you doing right now?"

Beth reached out and ran her hand across her comforter. "Not much. Just wallowing in self-pity."

Tiffany tsked. "Why? What's going on? Should I come over?"

Beth closed her eyes. "No, no. That's not necessary." She sighed, hating that she was being *that* friend right now. The one that lied to everyone. But it was for her mom. She could do this. "But enough about me. How was your trip?"

"I was just going to go to the Tavern. Want to join me? I'll tell you all about it."

Beth glanced out her window that overlooked the Braxtons' house, and the memory of seeing Josh washed over her again. "How come you didn't tell me that Josh was coming back?"

"Josh is back?"

Beth nodded. "Uh huh."

"Huh. Jonathan didn't say anything, but then again, he's been pretty busy, so we haven't talked in a while. Plus, me being gone probably didn't help. This must have been a recent development."

Tiffany worked as a receptionist for Braxton Construction as well as being Jonathan Braxton's (Josh's younger brother) best friend. He was literally the only guy Beth was okay with Tiffany abandoning her for.

"Did you see him?" Tiffany asked, her voice flirty.

Beth rolled her eyes. There were very few people who knew about her ridiculous crush on Josh. "Well, yes. But Mrs. Braxton was there. She invited me to dinner. I'm heading over there in an hour."

Tiffany said a very long "Ooo."

Beth sighed. "I should go."

"Okay," Tiffany said through her giggles.

They said their goodbyes, promising to get together soon, and Beth hung up. She set her phone down as her gaze made its way back over to the Braxton house. Curiosity won over and she got off the bed and sat down on the bench in front of her window that overlooked the Braxtons' front yard.

Her pulse quickened when she saw Josh standing by his truck. He had pulled a box up onto each shoulder and was making his way toward the garage apartment. A small boy who looked no older than five was following after him. She'd heard that he had a son, but that was about it. She didn't know his name or how old he was.

She allowed herself to wonder where Cindy was. Why would someone just allow their ex-husband to move out of the state with their son? He was a cute kid. Looked like a younger version of Josh. He even had a glove on and was throwing a baseball into it—just like Josh did the whole summer before seventh grade. He never took his glove off.

Josh paused and turned to say something to him. The little boy's shoulders slumped, and his steps slowed while Josh made his way over to the stairs that led to the above-garage apartment.

Beth watched as Josh glanced behind him a few times. She could see his expression soften as he set the boxes on the ground. He called to his son, and whatever he said made his son's whole face light up. He cheered and ran to the front yard, where he started throwing the ball up in the air.

Josh walked over to his truck and pulled open the passenger door. He emerged with a baseball glove and turned, calling something out. Seconds later, the ball whizzed through the air and smacked right into Josh's glove.

When Mrs. Braxton opened the front door and waved them in, Beth suddenly realized how late it was. She could only assume that Mrs. Braxton was calling them in for dinner, which meant if she didn't hurry, she was going to be late.

And right now, being around the Braxton family was the only thing she wanted to do.

Plus, it got her out of her house and away from the sadness the hung over everyone there like a black cloud.

After running a brush through her hair and touching up her makeup, she settled on a yellow sundress with white sandals.

She paused to glance at her reflection in the mirror and studied her outfit. Did it look like she was trying too hard? She wrinkled her nose. Probably.

But, she didn't have time to change. Hopefully, Mrs. Braxton wouldn't say anything about it. Sondra wasn't the most discreet person in Honey Grove. It was probably because she had been surrounded by men most of her life. She always said exactly what was on her mind.

Before Beth could talk herself into slipping into her pajamas and avoiding this whole night, she grabbed her purse, called a quick goodbye to her mom, and pulled the front door closed after her.

It took all of thirty seconds to cross the street and climb

the steps of the Braxton porch and knock three times on the door.

She stood there, holding her breath, as she waited for someone to answer.

The door opened and Josh appeared in the doorway.

It may have been her imagination, but she swore she saw his eyes light up when his gaze roamed over her.

"Hey, Beth," he said. He leaned on the door instead of moving to let her in.

"Hey, Josh," she said, praying her voice would come out normal.

He studied her for a moment and then glanced behind her. "Your parents coming?"

The familiar sinking feeling settled in her gut every time someone asked about her mom. It was a result of all the lies she'd been telling ever since she got back. And she hated it. "Mom's not feeling too good," she said. And then hurried to add, "Summer cold."

Josh studied her and then slowly nodded. "That's too bad. I was looking forward to saying hi."

Beth shrugged, praying they would get off the topic of her mother. "So, am I only admitted with a parent?"

Josh chuckled as he stepped back and let the door swing open. "Of course not. You're more than welcome."

Beth nodded and stepped into the room, trying hard not to notice that Josh didn't move when she came close. Instead, he remained right next to the door. She could smell his cologne and feel his presence.

Butterflies were dive-bombing her stomach. Thank goodness he couldn't hear the pounding of her heart right now.

She moved to slip off her sandals, and, just as she freed her heel from one of the straps, she lost her balance. Reaching out, she tried to stop herself, but two strong hands held onto her. One wrapped around her arm, and the other steadied her back.

"Whoa," Josh said.

Heat exploded throughout her body. Partially from his touch, but mostly from embarrassment. This was not how she'd dreamed of their reunion going.

"Are you okay?" he asked. His voice deeper than before.

She straightened, bringing herself inches from him. "Yep, mm-hmm," she said, forcing herself to meet his gaze.

He studied her for a moment and then, just as quickly as his touch had happened, he dropped his hands and pushed his fingers through his hair. "I'm, um, I'm sorry. I should probably go help Mom." He gave her a sheepish look before ducking his head and making his way into the kitchen.

Beth stood there, dumbfounded. Had she done something? She swallowed as she slipped off her shoes and set her purse on them. He was acting as if she had a disease.

Perhaps their connection earlier had all been in her mind.

And then she felt stupid.

Of course it had been in her mind. She was the one with the ridiculous crush on the neighbor boy, not the other way around. To Josh, she was just the annoying girl that had professed her love for him so many years ago.

He didn't have feelings for her and never would. Besides, she wasn't exactly marrying material—at least that's what Zander told her when he dumped her. And with her mom's illness, having any relationship was futile.

No. Josh being back wasn't some cosmic sign that they were meant to be together. It was just a coincidence she needed to not read into.

She'd been hurt before by misinterpreting a guy's intentions; she wasn't going to let that happen again.

She straightened her dress and forced a confident smile as she made her way across the living room and into the kitchen where she could hear voices.

Mr. Braxton, Josh, and Dean were sitting at the table. Dean waved hi, and Mr. Braxton shouted something at the TV as he slammed his hand down at the table.

Mrs. Braxton shushed him right before she said, "Beth! Thanks for joining us."

Beth nodded, but kept next to the wall. The Braxtons were such a warm and inviting family, but she couldn't help but feel out of place here.

When she glanced over at Josh, she noticed him watching her. He smiled and then turned his attention back to the TV.

Beth felt so confused. Why was he smiling and touching her one minute, then cold and distant the next? Was it just her complete inability to understand men? Or was there something more?

She let out her breath slowly. She was terrible at reading men, and she just needed to accept that Josh Braxton would never be interested in her like that. They'd known each other long enough; if something was going to start up, it would have.

She needed to realize that Josh was just going to be her friend, and that was all. Besides, her life was too complicated right now to bring anyone into it. It was better, for him and for her. She just needed to forget the feelings in her stomach. Too bad it was easier said than done.

THREE

JOSH

WAS it strange that he couldn't keep his gaze from slipping over to Beth every few seconds? Josh wanted to tell himself that it was normal and that he shouldn't read into it, but the more he studied Beth, the more he began to realize that she was no longer that little next door neighbor girl anymore.

She'd changed. And that intrigued him.

Then Jordan popped into his line of sight, and Josh turned to study his son, whose nose was wrinkled and his tongue was sticking out.

"What's up, JP?" he asked, grabbing his son and hoisting him up onto his lap.

Jordan buried his lips in Josh's ear. "This has broccoli in it," he whispered.

Josh glanced down at the casserole his mom had prepared.

After a few pokes with his fork, he found the offending food. He sighed. Leave it to Cindy to cater to Jordan's every whim. Instead of teaching their son to eat what he was given, Cindy had allowed him to pick and choose. Now Josh was left with Jordan's refusal to eat anything healthy.

"You'll be fine, bud," he said, giving Jordan a stern look. There was no way he had energy to fight Jordan over this. And he especially didn't want to fight with him in front of an audience.

"What's the problem?" Sondra asked, raising her gaze to study him.

"Nothing, Ma."

"This has broccoli," Jordan said, shoving his plate closer to his grandmother.

Sondra raised her eyebrows. "And you don't eat broccoli?"

Jordan shook his head and folded his arms. Josh wanted to crawl under the table to hide from the stares everyone was shooting his direction. It wasn't a secret that he had no idea what he was doing. He'd spent so much time studying in law school and then building his firm that he was rarely home. Now, he was left to figure out how to parent Jordan, alone.

He was so out of his depth that he was barely staying afloat. Most days, he was drowning.

"Well, Mr. Jordan, at Grandma's house, we don't tolerate picky eaters." Sondra folded her arms and stared his five-year-old down.

Jordan shifted on Josh's lap so he was facing his grandmother head on. "I don't eat broccoli," Jordan said, his voice dropping an octave. Josh winced. He knew what was going to happen next. Total melt down.

"That's too bad." Beth's quiet voice sounded from across the table.

Josh's gaze fell on her, surprised that she'd spoken. Jordan seemed to be just as shocked because he turned to stare at her too.

"Why?" Jordan asked.

Beth slowly picked up a piece of broccoli and studied it. "What's your favorite animal?"

Jordan hesitated before he said, "T-Rex."

A smile played on Beth's lips, and Josh couldn't help but stare at her. How had he never noticed that she was this beautiful?

Then Beth raised her gaze and, for a moment, held Josh's. He was pretty sure that everyone in the room could hear his heart hammering in his chest. Whoa. What was his problem?

She dropped her gaze to Jordan as she leaned in. "When I have to eat my broccoli, I like to pretend that I am a giant Tyrannosaurus rex, stomping through the jungle." She furrowed her brow and began moving her arms like she was a giant dinosaur.

Josh didn't need to glance down at his son to know that Jordan's eyes were most likely wide open. Anytime someone talked to him about dinosaurs, he was all in.

"And then I pretend that the broccoli pieces are trees."

Beth picked up her fork and glared at the broccoli. "It says, *please don't eat me.*" Beth flicked her gaze over to Jordan and wiggled her eyebrows. "But I don't care." She shoved the broccoli into her mouth while growling. Then she chewed dramatically and dropped her fork next to her plate. She leaned back and patted her tummy.

"I'm a big T-Rex. I eat everything," she said with a smile and a wink.

Josh smiled back. Was it wrong that he thought she was adorable? And the fact that she had his son completely enraptured made her even cuter.

Jordan turned around to look at Josh. He had a look in his eyes that said, *this lady is crazy.*

"Well, it's what *true* T-Rex fans do," Beth added.

Ooo, Beth was good. Setting the bait.

Jordan furrowed his brow as he turned back to Beth and folded his arms again. "I'm a true T-Rex fan."

Josh was skeptical that this would work, but he was willing to give it a shot. After all, she looked as if she knew what she was doing.

Jordan pushed off Josh's lap and slipped to the floor. Then he climbed back onto his chair and poked a few times at his broccoli. Then he growled and shoved one into his mouth, where he dramatically chewed it—just like Beth had done.

Beth cheered and clapped. Then she reached over the table to high-five him. "Great job, Jordan."

Jordan had swallowed by now and was looking pretty

proud of himself. "I did it, Dad," he said after slapping Beth's hand.

Josh tousled Jordan's hair. "Great job, buddy." He allowed his smile to remain as he turned his attention over to Beth, who raised her gaze up to meet his.

"Thank you," he mouthed.

It may have been his imagination, but he swore he saw her blush. "Of course," she whispered.

If he'd had a hard time not staring at her before, he was in deep trouble now. She returned to her quiet conversation with Dean, who was seated next to her.

"I think that settles it," Sondra said, loudly.

Everyone at the table turned to study his mom.

"What's settled?" Josh asked, furrowing his brow. What was his mom up to?

Sondra gave him a sly smile. "I was going to tell you that I was asked to help cook at the Honey Grove retirement center and won't be able to watch Jordan while you are at work."

Josh stared at his mom. Was she serious? Her promise to help with Jordan had been one of the reasons he came home. "What?"

"What's going on?" Jimmy asked, his deep voice booming through the room.

Sondra shot him a look, but Josh wasn't interested in whatever strange plot she was concocting. He couldn't work *and* watch Jordan. Why would his mom do this to him?

"Calm down, you two," Sondra said, glancing between Josh and his dad.

"Be calm, Ma? You told me you could help, and now you're saying you picked up a job at the retirement center?" He dropped against the back of his chair and let out his breath. Stress pressed down on his chest. What was he doing? He was an idiot if he thought he was fooling anyone about his capability to function.

"Right. But that's why I invited Beth over here." Sondra nodded at Beth, who had looked up with her brow furrowed.

Uh oh.

"She's looking for a job, and you need a nanny. It's a match made in heaven." Sondra practically sang out the last sentence.

Josh glanced over at Beth and gave her a small smile. "I'm sure you don't want to watch Jordan." This was not what Josh wanted. Sure, Beth was adorable and sweet with his son, but involving himself with anyone right then, even in this capacity, was not what he wanted.

He needed to get his life figured out before he invited anyone non-family into it. She deserved a sane and put-together boss. And that was not Josh. Not right now, anyway.

"I mean, you'd help Josh out, wouldn't you Beth?" Sondra asked.

Josh about fell out his chair. What was his mom doing?

Beth was studying her, and he saw her flick her gaze over to him before nodding. "Well, if he needs help, I'm happy to."

There was no way he could say no, now. Not when she said something like that. He furrowed his brow, angry at his mom for dragging Beth into this. "Are you sure? I mean, you must have better things to do with your time then help me out."

Beth drew her eyebrows together. "I'm, um..." She fiddled with her silverware. "It would actually really help me out, too."

Now it was Josh's turn to feel confused. Why would she need this job? She'd graduated from college. The last he'd heard, she was living in Pittsburgh with a career and a fiancé. Being a nanny seemed beneath her.

Josh shifted in his seat as he glanced down at his son, who was busily eating his broccoli like a T-Rex. Well, maybe it wouldn't be so bad, having her around. But, he knew she had more going for her than he did. He needed to make it clear that if she wanted out, she was more than welcome to leave. He didn't want her to feel like she was stuck helping him out.

"Well, let's do this for now. And if you find something better, I won't be disappointed." He gave her a wide smile and a wink. And then felt like an idiot. What was he doing? He was about to employ this woman. Flirting—or whatever he was doing—was pretty inappropriate.

Beth pinched her lips together and nodded. "Sure."

Sondra clapped her hands together and cheered. "Well, that just makes me happier than a dead pig in sunshine. I was sure I was going to be in big trouble, overbooking myself like that." She grinned at Josh, who tried not to shoot her an annoyed look.

Hadn't he just told her that he wasn't looking to bring people into his life right now—that he was a mess and it wasn't fair to bring anyone into his disaster zone?

But he should have known better. His mom always had a plan of her own, and she rarely changed it for anyone. His mom was going to get her way one way or the other. He really should be used to that by now.

Dinner wrapped up and, needing something to do, Josh grabbed his plate and declared that he would do the dishes. Once he was in the kitchen, he filled the sink with warm water. Just as he poured in some soap, causing bubbles to rise up, he heard his mom's voice from the other room.

"Be a dear and help Josh with the dishes."

Josh winced. Was she talking to Beth? Probably. And he wasn't sure how he felt about that. But he knew that he wasn't ready to decide how he felt about anyone other than his son.

Out of the corner of his eye, he saw Beth walk into the kitchen. She tucked her hair behind her ears and glanced around. He wished he could read the look on her face. Was she happy? Sad? Frustrated? She was their guest, and yet his mom had no problem employing her in more ways than one.

"Wanna dry?" he asked, grabbing a dish towel and holding it out.

She studied it and then took it from him. "Sure. I mean, if that's okay."

Confused, Josh kept his gaze on her for moment longer than he should have. But then he scolded himself and shrugged. "Of course. I hate dishes. I need all the help I can get."

She chuckled. The sound was soft and melodic. And he liked it. Was it bad that he wanted to hear it again?

He turned back to the sink and dunked a stack of plates into the water. Beth stepped up to the counter and waited as he washed the first one. After it was clean, he handed it over to her. For a brief moment, her fingers brushed his, and sparks of electricity shot up his arm.

It surprised him so much that he almost dropped the plate back into the sink. Thankfully, Beth had a good grasp on it. After she rinsed it off and dried it, she disappeared to stack it in a cupboard.

They worked in silence for a few minutes. The quiet was killing him.

"Are you happy to be back?" he asked, turning to study her.

It wasn't until now that he realized how close they really were. She was inches from him as she stood there, rinsing a cup.

She shrugged. "I guess. I mean, it's good for me to be back. It was needed..." she said, her voice trailing off.

Josh furrowed his brow. What did that mean?

She glanced over at him and pinched her lips together. That reaction intrigued him. Was she hiding something? When their eyes met, he saw something there—hurt? He wasn't sure, but for some reason, all he wanted to do was figure out what it was.

"What about you?" she asked as she grabbed another cup and rinsed it off.

Josh wanted to jump back to talking about her. To ask what was bothering her. But it wasn't his place. Sure, they'd grown up together, but that didn't mean she had to tell him all her problems.

So he sucked in his breath as all the feelings about his move and his ex-wife flooded his systems. "Not how I saw my life going," he said as pain jabbed his ribs. Why couldn't he be strong enough to be okay with this? Cindy was a horrible person. He should have expected she'd do some-thing like cheat on him and leave him.

He saw Beth nod as she dried a cup. "I get that."

When he turned to look at her, his heart sped up. There was a look of understanding in her eyes. Like she knew what failure felt like. For the first time in a long time, he felt as if someone else understood what he was going through. He felt a connection with Beth that he hadn't thought he would find here in Honey Grove.

Sure, there was attraction there, but what he was feeling was something more. She knew what it was like to have her entire life turned upside-down.

Coming back to Honey Grove was the last thing she'd wanted as well. But, as life always does, it decided to make a joke of them, so here they were, drying dishes in the kitchen of his childhood home.

He couldn't help but smile at her. "Well, Beth, I'm glad we're back here, together."

Her eyebrows rose as she studied him. He pinched his lips together when he realized how that must sound. "I mean, it's nice to have friends around," he hurried to tag on.

Her cheeks blushed as she took the mixing bowl from him. "Friends," she said softly.

He nodded as she finished drying the bowl and slipped it into the cupboard behind him. They worked in silence until Beth got a call on her phone and she excused herself, saying that she was needed at home.

Josh nodded at her and couldn't help but watch as she walked from the room. There was something different about her that intrigued him.

"See you tomorrow?" he asked her retreating frame.

She paused just inside the door. Then she turned and smiled at him. "Definitely."

He nodded and she gave him a small wave as she disappeared. As he turned back to the sink, excitement bubbled in his chest. He didn't care if it was wrong—he was excited to see her again, tomorrow. For the first time ever, he wanted to thank his mom for interfering. Maybe she was right. Perhaps Beth was who he needed right now.

If anything, she wouldn't ask him incessant questions.

Even though he didn't really know her anymore, he suspected that she knew just what he was going through. And right now, he needed someone like that in his life.

FOUR

BETH

BETH WOKE up the next morning feeling excited and terrified at the same time. She swallowed as she stared up at the ceiling while the early morning light lit up her room. Thoughts of Josh and their conversations yesterday flooded into her mind.

She was working for Josh Braxton—the guy she'd crushed on for as long as she could remember.

Not only was she going to see him every day, but she'd talk to him, take care of his son, and be in his home.

Sighing, she covered her eyes with her arm. What was she doing? Was she an idiot? Did she think that working for Josh would make him realize what he'd been missing out of his whole life and come rushing to declare his love for her?

Ugh.

The lightening of her stomach, and the fact that her

heart was picking up speed, told her that was exactly what she thought.

Her phone buzzed, the alarm finally ringing. Not wanting to sit in bed and dwell on her stupidity, she pulled off the covers and headed straight into the bathroom. Maybe if she busied herself with getting ready, she wouldn't have time to convince herself to cancel on Josh.

Right now, the thought of being around him terrified her more than the thought of not having a job.

After she was cleaned and dressed, she settled on an off-the-shoulder peasant top and cut-off shorts. After slipping on her sandals, she threw her hair back in a braid, dabbed a bit of makeup on her face—not enough that made her look like she was trying—and headed out of her room.

Her mom was sitting in the living room when Beth got downstairs. Her shoulders were slumped and her eyes were drifting closed and then back open as the voice of a news-caster carried from the TV. Beth tiptoed past the chair and into the kitchen, where she grabbed a banana.

After eating it along with a container of yogurt, she headed back into the living room to check on her mom before leaving. Just as she adjusted the blanket on her mom's lap, Joanne's eyes fluttered open. Beth gave her a small smile as she reached over and grabbed a footrest from the other side of the chair.

"Where are you going?" Joanne asked. Her forehead furrowed as she studied Beth's face.

Beth glanced up at her mom as she carefully lifted her

feet and set them on the footstool. "I told you. I'm the nanny for Josh now."

Butterflies took flight in her stomach. She muscled them down as much as she could, but they were persistent little buggers.

Joanne reached out and grasped Beth's hand. Her expression had morphed into one of panic. "You won't...I mean, don't say anything," her mom rasped.

Beth hated how secretive they were being about this. She could think of a lot of people in the community who would be more than happy to help out her family. But, if it was her mother's wish, it was the least Beth could do.

So she nodded. "Of course. Mum's the word." She lifted her finger to her lips.

Her mom settled back into the chair and let out a breath. "Good." With that, she let her eyes drop closed.

Taking this as her cue to leave, Beth grabbed a glass of water and an applesauce from the kitchen and set it on the side table next to her mom. After adjusting the volume on the TV so Joanne could sleep, she grabbed her purse and slipped out of the house.

It took all of a minute to cross the road and climb the steps that ran up the side of the garage. She paused just outside of the door to Josh's apartment. She took a few deep breaths and then reached up and knocked.

The muffled sound of cartoons could be heard from where she stood, along with Josh's voice.

"Get the door, JP," he shouted.

Just from the tone of his voice, she could tell that he was stressed. Instantly, she felt bad. It was her job to lighten his load, and yet she had spent so much time getting ready that he was now irritated.

The lock clicked and the door opened. Jordan stood there in his superhero pajamas, staring up at her.

"What are you doing here?" he asked.

Beth smiled. She couldn't help it. She liked Jordan. "I'm here to hang out with you."

Jordan wrinkled his nose. "I don't need a babysitter."

She shrugged. "Good. 'Cause that's not what I am. I just promised your dad that I would spend some time with you while he goes to work."

Jordan studied her a bit longer and then shrugged as he held up a remote tucked in one hand. "My show is playing."

Beth nodded as he turned and headed into the small living room to the right. He jumped a few times on the worn leather couch before settling in. Taking this as her invitation to come in, Beth stepped inside.

The Braxton's hadn't updated the furniture in this apartment in ages, but it was clean and homey. She took a deep breath as she slipped off her purse and set it next to her sandals by the door. To the left was the kitchen. It was small. Two main countertops, a refrigerator, and a small stove filled the room.

It probably didn't matter, though. Mrs. Braxton would be insulted if Josh decided to eat here. She walked along the outskirts of the room, running her fingers along the smooth countertops.

"You're here," Josh's deep, playful voice filled her ears and caused her to shiver.

She swallowed, hoping to squelch the feelings that had risen up inside of her, and turned. "Yeah. I'm sorry. I can come earlier tomorrow."

Josh looked as if he'd just stepped out of the shower. His hair was damp, and she could smell hints of his mint shampoo. He was wearing a dark blue t-shirt and jeans. He ran his hands through his hair. "I think I can manage."

Beth eyed him. Even though he looked put together, she could see a hint of stress lingering around his eyes. She could only imagine what he was going through. At least when Zander had dumped her, all she had to worry about was herself. Throwing a kid into that equation had to be rough.

She gave him a small smile. "Well, I'm just a phone call and a minute sprint away."

Josh chuckled. "It would take you a minute to sprint here?"

Heat raced across her skin, and she was pretty sure it settled in her cheeks. Josh's gaze moved to her face. His teasing look turned into an apologetic one, and it made her feel terrible.

"It's okay. Everyone here knows I'm the slow one in the Johnson family."

Josh nodded just as an alarm filled the air. He reached

behind him and grabbed his phone. "Crap. I'm late." He glanced up at her. "Any questions?" he asked as he made his way over to the door and slipped on his boots.

Beth nodded. "Allergies?"

"None."

"Eating time?"

Josh's gaze made its way over to Jordan whose head was peeking up over the back of the couch. "He's good at letting you know. And if that doesn't work, whenever you eat, he'll eat."

"Great. Anything else you want us to do?"

Josh finished lacing up his shoes. "Just keep him alive?"

Beth nodded, a laugh escaping her lips. "I can do that."

Josh grabbed his keys off the hook next to the door. He twisted them around his fingers. "Well, I should be back by five. We're remodeling a few Honey Grove homes."

Beth nodded again, and then felt like an idiot. Couldn't she come up with any other reaction when he spoke? "No worries. Whenever you get home, you get home. I'm sure we'll have a blast."

Josh studied her for a moment longer, and then he smiled. "Thanks for doing this, Beth. I really wasn't sure what I was going to do."

Beth shrugged. "It's not a big deal. Really. Besides, you're helping me out. I've been looking for a job, and to have one so close to home..." She pinched her lips together. What was the matter with her? Was she crazy? Ten minutes in and she was about to spill everything to Josh. She cleared her throat and forced a relaxed look—or a semblance of one. "It's just good to have a plan."

Josh held her gaze, and, for a moment, she could see that he wasn't sure if he believed her. But the last thing she wanted to do was break her promise to her mom, so she just smiled.

"You should probably get going. You don't want to be late on your first day." She nodded at the door. There was a tug of war going on inside of her. She wanted him to stay but feared what she might say if he did. It was better for everyone if he just left.

Josh's gaze flicked over to the clock on the microwave, and he nodded. "Yeah. I should go." He turned and went over to the couch, where he dipped down and pressed his lips to the top of Jordan's head. "I'm leaving, squirt. Beth's here. Listen to her."

Jordan shifted and complained about being interrupted. Josh tousled his hair and then made his way over to the door. "Call if you need me. My number's on the fridge."

Beth glanced over at the fridge to see that a piece of torn paper had been tacked to it. She nodded. "Got it. I'm sure we'll be fine."

Josh smiled, pulled open the door, and gave her one final wave. Once he was gone, the only sound that filled the air was the TV.

Not sure what to do, Beth paced back and forth before finding herself over at the couch. "Hungry?" she asked.

Jordan looked up at her for a brief moment before

returning his attention to the TV. "Yeah. But I need my Reese's Puffs."

"Reese's Puffs," Beth repeated as she moved over to the kitchen and pulled open the cupboards. Besides some condiment packs, she found no food.

Not sure what to do, she sighed. "Have you guys gone grocery shopping?" she asked to the top of Jordan's head.

When he didn't answer, she assumed he either didn't know or didn't care. He was only five after all. But mayonnaise and ketchup packets weren't going to suffice as breakfast. She walked over to the TV and stood next to it.

"How about we go into town today? We can get you guys some groceries and maybe stop at the park?"

Jordan ignored her until she said park. Suddenly, she was much more interesting than the hamburger that was dancing across the screen. "Does it have a slide?"

Beth was pretty sure it did. But it'd been a while since she'd been there. Most parks had slides, right?

"Yes."

He narrowed his eyes. "And swings?"

"Yes," she said not meaning to drag out every letter of the word. If she was wrong, she'd feel bad.

Jordan studied her for a moment longer before he shrugged and scooted off the couch. "I guess I'll go."

Grateful that she wasn't going to have to drag him from the apartment, Beth walked over to the door and slipped on her sandals.

A few minutes later, Jordan returned wearing an orange

t-shirt and shorts. He grabbed his flip-flops and wiggled his toes until they were on.

Beth slung her purse onto her shoulder and reached out to grab the door handle.

"Wait," Jordan said and ran into the back bedroom.

Beth paused as she watched him disappear. It didn't take long for him to return with a stuffed gorilla in one arm.

"Can Captain come?" he asked as he hugged the animal to his chest.

Beth smiled. "Sure." After she opened the door, she waved Jordan through.

The warming morning air surrounded her as she stepped out after him. She pulled the door closed and followed Jordan down the stairs. Beth walked next to Jordan on the driveway as she led him to her car.

"Where are you two off to?" Sondra's voice made Beth yelp. She glanced over to see Josh's mom standing there with two brown paper bags.

Beth smiled. "We're heading into town. Josh has no groceries, and Jordan wants to play at the park."

Sondra reached out and smothered Jordan in hugs and kisses. Jordan didn't seem to appreciate that. He was wiggling and pushing away from her. Beth was having a hard time trying to keep from laughing at Jordan's scrunched nose and stuck out tongue.

"Nana," he said when he finally pulled free.

Sondra just shrugged and turned to Beth. "Josh and Mr.

Braxton forgot their lunch. Could you be a dear and bring these to them?"

Beth's heart began to beat harder at the thought of seeing Josh again. It was ridiculous. She needed to get a handle on this, especially if she was going to be working for him. Realizing that she was taking way too long to respond to Mrs. Braxton, Beth nodded and held out her hand for the bags.

There was no way she wanted to give the busy-body of Honey Grove any inclination that she had a crush on her son. "Yeah. Sure. Do you know where they are working today?"

Sondra furrowed her brow. "I think they are remodeling Tricia Young's house. Ever since that jerk left her, she's been trying to erase everything he ever touched."

And there it was. When Sondra Braxton knew something about you, she had a tendency to spill it.

Beth just nodded and slipped the paper bags into her purse. "Got it. We'll stop by there on our way to the Pick 'n Save."

Sondra nodded, a satisfied look on face. Like she'd just accomplished a secret task. Even though Beth wasn't thrilled to see Tricia Young—the resident rich lady of Honey Grove and former homecoming queen—she knew that sticking around Mrs. Braxton always spelled trouble. And she didn't want to dwell too much on dissecting Sondra's alternative motive.

Jordan had distracted himself over by the grass. When

she got closer to him, she saw that he was studying a row of ants coming from a hill.

"Ready?"

Jordan glanced up and nodded. "Yep."

"I'll see you later, Mrs. B."

"Of course," Mrs. Braxton said with a wave.

When Beth and Jordan got to the end of the driveway, Mrs. Braxton called out for her to stop. When Beth turned, she saw that Mrs. Braxton was carrying a booster seat in her hand. As Beth took it from her, Mrs. Braxton held onto it for a moment longer, locking her gaze with Beth's. "Thanks for doing this. You've been a godsend to Josh."

Heat raced across her skin as Beth nodded. "No problem."

Then she held on to Jordan's arm as they walked across the street and over to her car. Once Jordan was buckled in, Beth climbed into the driver's seat and settled in.

She took a deep breath as she started the engine. She needed to take a moment to prepare herself. It was what you needed to do when it came to Tricia Young.

FIVE

JOSH

JOSH TOOK a deep breath as he turned off his truck and slipped his keys into the glove compartment. He'd been to enough job sites to know that keeping his keys in his pocket was a recipe for disaster. Besides, this was Honey Grove. No one was going to steal his truck.

He shifted in his seat as he opened the driver's door and dropped to the ground. The beautiful log cabin in front of him sported the name *Braxton Construction* across the top. A feeling of nostalgia rose in his chest.

He crossed the parking lot, the crunch of gravel filling his ears. Not much had changed—not even the material on the ground. He'd spent so many years here, helping his dad plot construction plans or waiting for his dad to finish so they could go to a job site. It was like reliving his childhood all over again.

Cool air blasted from inside as he stepped into the small

room where Tiffany Sounders sat. She was Johnathan's best friend and had been working for Braxton Construction for the last few years.

"Tiffany," Josh shouted as he spread out his arms

"Josh," she exclaimed as she pushed away from the desk. She wrapped her arms around him and he pulled her up into a twirl. She'd been around so much growing up that he thought of her as a little sister.

Once he set her back down, she slugged his shoulder. "So you came back," she said, tucking her dark brown hair behind her ear.

Josh shrugged. "Honey Grove is like the mother ship. Eventually all the little ships must return."

She pulled an exaggerated contemplative look. "I never thought of it like that."

Josh laughed as he pointed toward his dad's office. "He in there?"

She nodded. "Yep. On the phone. He should be out in a minute. You guys are late for the Young remodel."

"Young?"

"Yep. Tricia Young is remodeling her house. Again." She stuck out her tongue.

Tricia Young. Huh. Josh hadn't thought about her since leaving Honey Grove. They'd been prom king and queen senior year, and half their graduating class had predicted they would end up married.

But she married Marcus Young, the town's rich kid, and

Josh moved to Colorado. Funny how life can bring two people back together after so long.

"She still married to Marcus?" Josh asked, settling into the chair that faced Tiffany's desk.

Tiffany sat back down and was fidgeting with a pen. "You didn't hear?" she asked as she leaned in.

"Hear what?"

"Marcus left. Ditched her for some twenty-year-old nanny. Guess they had some non-cheat clause in their prenup, which he broke. She got the money and the house, and he got Barbie." She pulled a disgusted face and Josh couldn't help but laugh.

And then he felt bad laughing about the misfortunes of the people in this town. Especially when it hit so close to home. "That's terrible."

Tiffany gave him a *no it's not* look. "Catch up with Tricia and then come back and tell me that."

Josh furrowed his brow. What did that mean? But before he could ask, his dad's door opened and Jimmy stepped out. "Tiffany, call the Van Burens. The cupboards they sent us were all built an inch too short. We can't use them. Tell them we demand a discount and I'll need them by next week."

Josh glanced over at Tiffany, who was furiously taking notes. "On it, Boss," she said as she picked up the phone, dialing before Jimmy could draw breath.

"You made it," his dad said, drawing Josh's attention back over to him.

Josh stood and crossed the room to shake his dad's hand. "Of course. I'm ready to dive back into the family business. At least for a while."

Jimmy studied him for a moment before a huge smile spread across his lips. "I'm happy to have you back, son. We're late for the Young residence, but let me show you what I've been working on." He clapped his hand on Josh's shoulder and led him into the office. "You're going to love this."

JOSH HAD to wrangle Jimmy away from his plans so that they wouldn't be any later than they already were. Jimmy didn't seem to mind the fact that Tricia had called at least ten times asking where they were. He was perfectly content to sit there and talk shop.

After he had to practically stuff Jimmy into the passenger side of his dad's pickup, he climbed in and started up the engine. Tiffany stepped out of the office and gave them a final wave as he backed out of the parking lot.

It was strange, driving the back roads of his home town. New buildings had come up, and yet, everything felt the same. It was a small town. You could drive from one side to the other in about fifteen minutes. Small shops lined the downtown roads, and Josh waved at a few people who were out sitting under the shade or watering their plants.

They looked surprised to see him at first, then they

shouted greetings, saying it was good he was home. Once they were through downtown, Josh started up the long roads to the richer parts of Honey Grove. Where Tricia lived.

The roads began to wind, and the foliage crept up around them. It was hard to believe that the ocean was just a thirty-minute drive away. His GPS announced that they had arrived just as Josh pulled into a long, winding driveway. He came to a stop at the wrought iron gates, letting his truck idle there as he rolled his window down and pressed the button on the black box that was perched next to his window.

He waited, and suddenly Tricia's voice blared through the speaker. "Um, yes? Hello?"

"Hey, Tricia, it's Josh. We're finally here," he said. For some reason, the panic in her voice made him smile. Looking at her house, he wondered what on earth she had to feel panicked about.

"Right. Josh," she said, dragging out every letter of his name.

He gave the speaker a funny look as he tried to decipher her intentions. He shifted in his seat. "We'd like to get started, so if you can open the gates, we'll get to work."

"Right, of course. Come on in." There was a buzzing sound as the gates began to swing open.

Josh pulled in to the large roundabout driveway. A fountain sat in the middle of the grass, with water shooting from the mouth of four fish. He couldn't help but shake his head. Tricia had some crazy money.

"Get ready, son," Jimmy said as he pulled his door open. "This lady can be a bit crazy."

Josh chuckled. Oh, he knew. She'd always been drama in high school, and he doubted that she'd be any different in her thirties. "It's okay, Dad. I'm sure I can handle Tricia."

Jimmy just scoffed as he climbed out of the truck and slammed the door, muttering under his breath, "Don't say I didn't warn you."

Josh got out and slammed the door, following his dad up to the doors, which opened almost instantly. Josh glanced over at his dad. He looked just as startled as Josh felt.

"Josh Braxton," Tricia said in a high-pitched, squealing voice. Suddenly, her arms wrapped around him, and he was sandwiched against her chest. Her hair was blonder and her tan deeper than he remembered. She was wearing a floral mini dress and four inch heels.

"Hey, Tricia," Josh said as he pulled back to look down at her.

Her wide blue eyes peered up at him. "It's so good to see you." She dropped her arms, but not before she found his hand and squeezed it.

Josh's gaze dropped to their clasped hands, but, before he could do anything about it, she let go and stepped back. He ran his hand through his hair, forcing himself not to think about what had just happened.

"So, you're doing some remodeling?" he asked, not sure what he was supposed to say.

"I'm going to go check on the work. Catch up with you later?" Jimmy asked as he took a step forward.

Josh shot him a *help me* look but Jimmy just chuckled as he disappeared down one of the many halls.

Tricia linked arms with Josh, clearly missing his discomfort, and began dragging him through the foyer and into the living room off to the left. Her heels clicked on the marble floor. Sunlight seeped through the large picture widows and glimmered off the chandelier above them. He couldn't imagine how they could make this home better. It was breathtaking.

"I'm having my pool redone, my kitchen expanded, and my master bedroom doubled in square footage. I'm tired of living in cramped quarters."

Josh couldn't help the scoff that escaped his lips. He'd categorize this house as a lot of things, but cramped was not one of them. Tricia looked hurt as she glanced up at him. Not wanting to lose this job for his dad, Josh tried to backtrack.

"What I mean is it's a beautiful home. I can't imagine how we could make it better."

She studied him before she giggled. "You're right. But everything can be improved upon." The way she flourished her hand in front of her body made Josh wonder if she was talking about the house or herself. He wasn't really sure how he was supposed to respond to that.

"Come on, let me show you the backyard."

She tugged on his arm and led him through the half torn

down kitchen, through one of the three sliding doors, and out to a huge backyard. The pool was in shambles, and a very disgruntled boy sat in an inflatable pool in the yard with his arms folded.

"Mom," he whined, flicking water in her direction.

"Not now, Tanner," she said, shooting him a stern look and then turning to smile at Josh. "Sorry. Tanner is my son, and he's not too happy with my choice of renovations."

Josh studied Tanner. He didn't look any older than Jordan. "How old is he?"

"Five. Going to kindergarten this year. I can't wait." She leaned into Josh and nudged his shoulder. "I mean, I normally have a nanny watch him, but she's having surgery, and I can't find a replacement."

Josh glanced over at her. Wow. He was grateful that he had Beth. Which reminded him, he should probably call and check in. He took out his phone to see if she'd tried to call him. No new notifications.

"Why are you so interested in my son?" Tricia said, drawing his attention back to her.

Josh shrugged. "No big reason." He sighed as he pushed his hand through his hair. "I have a son as well."

The smile that emerged on Tricia's lips both intrigued and scared him.

"Really?"

He nodded.

"That's fantastic." She got a strange, far off look for a moment before snapping her gaze back to him. "I'm sorry."

Her expression turned sheepish. "I do that sometimes. Mom brain."

He nodded, not sure how to respond to anything Tricia said. She didn't seem to notice, instead she just giggled. There was a nervous hint to it. "Well, I should get back inside. Phone calls won't answer themselves."

Josh nodded and glanced over at Tanner who was blowing bubbles in the water. Should she just leave him unattended?

"He'll be fine. He's been taking swimming lessons since he could crawl."

Josh shot her a smile, but her lack of concern made him uncomfortable. Maybe he'd take the job of breaking up the pool so he could keep an eye on him.

"I'll see you at break?" Tricia asked.

The flirty tone to her voice threw Josh a bit. He hadn't tried to date anyone since Cindy. And the truth was, he wasn't even sure how. They'd been together for so long that, now she was gone, he feared the mess he'd become.

"Sure. If I take one," he said. Work seemed like a good distraction right now.

Tricia's laugh was high-pitched and loud as she swatted his arm. Then she charged off to the house. Now alone with Tanner, Josh squinted over at the boy who was half submerged in the water like a crocodile, studying him.

He shot him a wave as he wandered over to the jack-hammer that was resting against the wall of the pool house. He got out his phone and texted his dad that he was going to get started on demolition for the pool. Jimmy responded with a thumbs up.

After donning a pair of safety glasses and getting everything situated, Josh turned the jackhammer on and got started. The machine roared to life as he began to break up the concrete and tile at the top of the pool.

Thirty minutes later, movement next to him drew his attention. A few feet away stood Beth. She was waving her hands, trying to get his attention. Panic coursed through his veins as he flipped the jackhammer off. His hands were numb, but he didn't care.

"Where's Jordan?" were the first words from his mouth.

Beth had parted her lips to say something, but then stopped. She paused as if she were processing what he'd said, and then her expression morphed into regret.

"I'm so sorry. Jordan is fine. He's over there." She waved over to the inflatable pool. Jordan was talking to Tanner, who'd gotten out a giant pool shark that took up half the space inside his tiny pool.

His heart returned to normal speed at the sight of his son. He took a deep breath and blew it out. "Sorry. I wasn't expecting you here, so I figured..." He let his voice trail off. He was an idiot. He hoped she didn't think that he didn't trust her with watching his son. That, on the first day, he already suspected something disastrous had happened.

"I'm sorry. I should have texted before." Her voice had grown quiet, and she dropped her gaze.

Great. He needed to apologize. "Hey, it's okay. I probably wouldn't have even heard with the jackhammer going. I guess I'm just one of those panicky parents." He reached out and grabbed her hand, hoping she'd look up at him.

Her gaze whipped up to his and then down to their hands.

Whoa. That might have been a mistake. "Sorry," he muttered as he dropped his hand.

Beth shook her head. "No, it's okay." Then she glanced up at him. "I was just dropping off your lunch. Sondra insisted."

Josh chuckled. Of course. That was so his mother. "Thanks," he said and then glanced around. "Where is it?"

Beth motioned toward the sliding glass doors. "Tricia said she'd put them in the fridge for you."

Josh nodded. "Perfect."

Beth chewed her lip. "Well, I'm taking Jordan to the park and then to the grocery store. You have no food in your house."

Embarrassment flooded Josh's veins as he thought back to this empty kitchen. He should have prepared better. "I'm so sorry." He began to reach into his back pocket and pull out his wallet. "You can just get lunch for yourself and Jordan. I'll pay. And you shouldn't have to buy my groceries."

Beth shook her head but took the hundred he handed her. "It's okay. I'm happy to help."

Their fingers brushed again, and the same tingling sensation rushed up his arm. He cleared his throat as if somehow that would erase this strange connection he felt toward Beth.

She tucked the money into her purse and smiled at him. "Well, you should get back to work, and I've got things to do."

Josh nodded. That was probably best. With Beth gone, these strange feelings that seemed to creep up inside of his chest every time he saw her would go away.

He hoped.

SIX

BETH

BETH'S MIND swam as she crossed the yard and made her way into the house by way of the large sliding glass doors that made up the back of the house. She called to Jordan just before she slipping into the chilly, air-conditioned room. Jordan waved to Tanner and came inside.

Beth shut the door behind him, the heat of the day still lingering around her.

"Get everything figured out?" Tricia asked. She was sitting on a barstool in the kitchen with a glass of wine in front of her. She looked tired. After having spent an hour with Jordan, Beth was beginning to understand why.

She wasn't even Jordan's mom and she was tired—she could only imagine what it would be like to be single parent.

"Yes. Thanks," she said, shooting Tricia a sympathetic smile.

Tricia nodded and picked up her champagne flute and

took a sip from it. Then she shot Beth a sheepish look. "Juice," she said, waving toward the deep red liquid. "If I drink it from the wine glass it helps me pretend that it's the real thing."

Feeling stupid that Beth just automatically assumed it was wine, she gave Tricia a big smile. "I totally get that."

Tricia traced her finger along the tip of the glass as she got a far off look in her eye. "Things have just been hard since Tanner's dad left. I just don't know what to do anymore." She sighed as she leaned forward on her hand and began rubbing her temples. "I just never thought I'd be going at this alone."

Realizing that Tricia needed some support, Beth grabbed the barstool that was right next to her and pulled it out. She sat down and then reached her arm around Tricia's shoulders and gave her a squeeze. "I totally get that. Life has a way of kicking us when we already feel down."

Tricia tipped her head toward Beth and studied her. Then she pinched her lips together and Beth could see the tears brimming on her lids. Tricia took a deep breath and reached out to fiddle with the glass again.

"I guess I just thought I'd eventually figure this all out. But I'm drowning. And now, my nanny quit, and I'm all alone."

Beth thought back to the gardener and maid she'd walked past on her way into the house, never mind the hoard of men wandering around working on renovations.

She wouldn't call Tricia alone. But, maybe that's how she truly felt.

"I've wanted to get more work done, but it's impossible without someone to watch Tanner." She shot Beth a hopeful look.

What was she getting at?

"What happened to your other nanny?" She wasn't sure why she asked, she just couldn't help it. Tricia was like a vortex, pulling people in despite their better judgement.

Tricia took another deep breath, exaggerating the movement in her shoulders. "She had a baby. Quit on me. Just like everyone else," she wailed.

Beth chewed her lip as she tried to force the next words down. There was no way she wanted to say what was on the tip of her tongue.

"All I need is someone to help me with him a few days a week. At least until I can find another nanny." Tricia turned to Beth, her eyes wide and desperate.

"I—um..." Was Tricia really asking her to nanny Tanner as well? "Well, I'd have to check with Josh first. But if he's okay with it, I can't imagine why I wouldn't be able to take on Tanner as well."

Tricia squealed and wrapped her arms around Beth. "You are a saint, you know that? I mean, I was desperate and in need, and you just showed up and relieved my worries." She pulled back, and the desperation and worry that had plagued her gaze seemed to have vanished.

Beth studied her, feeling a bit whiplashed from her

change in emotions. But before she could even wonder what that meant, Jordan came up next to her and patted her arm.

"Are we going to the park now?" he asked. His eyes were wide and innocent.

Beth glanced down at him and nodded. "Of course. Let's go."

"You're going to the park?" Tricia asked.

Beth nodded, hoping that Tricia wasn't going to ask her to bring Tanner along. It was her first day of watching Jordan, and she was still trying to get her bearings. "Um, yeah."

"Oh, Tanner loves the park. You won't mind?"

Beth studied her and then sighed as she nodded. "Sure. Why not. I'm sure Jordan would love someone to play with."

Jordan's enthusiastic nod told her that she'd surmised correctly.

"Great. Let me grab him and you can go," Tricia called over her shoulder as she made her way through the back doors.

Beth took a deep breath. She could do this. After all, how hard could two five-year-olds be? Plus, it was extra money, and that was definitely something she needed right now.

If those were the positives, was it wrong that she felt so hopeless? How had her life come to this?

The sliding door opened. Almost instantly, her heart picked up speed. Josh stepped into the kitchen, and the smile on his face almost made her body melt. His cheeks were pink from the heat, and sweat glistened across his brow. Dust from the tile he'd been scrapping covered his hair and clothes. Someone so dirty shouldn't look so good.

"Hey, you're still here," he said, walking gingerly over to the cupboard and grabbing out a glass.

Beth nodded, suddenly forgetting how to speak. "Yeah, Tricia cornered me. Asked me if I could watch Tanner for her until she found another nanny."

Josh had been filling up his glass with water while studying her. His eyebrows went up as he brought it to his lips and downed the water in a few swallows. Once it was empty, he set it in the sink. "Wow. Well, how do you feel about that?"

Beth shrugged as she reached out and brushed her fingers across the cool marble countertops. "I was actually going to ask what you thought about it. After all, I did give you my word that I'd watch Jordan. If you don't want me to divide my focus, I can say no."

Josh folded his arms as he stared at Beth. She tried not to notice how the muscles in his forearms rippled from the movement. She also tried to ignore the intensity in his stare. What was he thinking? Did she want to know?

"It's up to you," he said. "I mean, it's probably going to pay well." He unfolded his arms and motioned to Tricia's house. "Plus, that means you'll probably be hanging out here as well." He winked at her and her heart picked up speed.

Hoping her cheeks didn't look as flushed as they felt, Beth just smiled. "I guess that is an advantage."

Josh's smile wavered as he studied her. Before they could continue their conversation, Tricia came into the kitchen, red-faced and grumbling. She had a firm hand on Tanner's arm and was dragging him behind her.

"You're going to the park," she said, turning to stare down at Tanner.

Tanner was a cute kid, even though it looked as if he were giving his mom a run for her money. His loose blond curls cascaded across his forehead, and his bright blue eyes stared at Beth in a challenging sort of way.

This was going to be interesting.

"Ms. Beth, Tanner. Tanner, Ms. Beth," Tricia said, motioning between the two of them. Beth gave him a smile. All he did was stare back at her.

Tricia dipped down so she could meet Tanner's eyes. "You listen to Ms. Beth, do you hear? No more running off."

Beth's ears perked up. So, he was a runner. She was going to have to remember that.

Tanner didn't acknowledge Tricia as she gave him a few more commands and then led him over to where Beth stood.

"I'll pay a thousand a week until I find a new nanny," Tricia said, her eyes wide in desperation.

Beth tried to prevent her jaw from dropping, but from the satisfied look on Tricia's face, her reaction was good enough. Right now, a thousand dollars would make such a difference for Beth and her mom. "Um, sure. I guess I can work with that."

Movement behind Tricia drew Beth's attention to Josh,

who was shooting her a thumbs up. Beth smiled and dropped her attention to Tanner. He was laying on the ground, kicking the barstool next to him.

"Ready to go to the park?" she asked.

Tanner glanced up at her and shrugged.

"It'll be fun," Beth tried again, reaching down to help him stand. He kept his body limp, which required Beth to heave him up onto her shoulder. "I guess we better get this sack of potatoes to the car," she said, smiling down at Jordan.

"Yay," he cheered as he followed after Beth.

They walked through the front door and out to her car, the early afternoon heat surrounding them. She let out her breath as she dumped Tanner into the booster seat that Tricia had the gardener bring out to her and buckled him in. He didn't protest, but he also didn't move to help her.

Once everyone was situated, Beth pulled out of the driveway and onto the road. This was going to be interesting. She had a feeling that her once normal life was about to change drastically.

———

SWEAT CLUNG to Beth's body as she wrangled Tanner into his seat and shut the door. Complicated didn't even begin to describe this kid. He refused to listen, ran after a guy with a dog, and disappeared from view for a good fifteen minutes before Beth found him wading into a nearby creek.

After buckling him into his seat, she slammed the door

and collapsed against the car, taking a deep breath to calm her nerves. Jordan was staring up at her. The expression on his face mimicked her sentiments. What the heck was wrong with that kid?

"Let's go, buddy," she said, pushing away the hair that clung to her face and mustering a smile.

Jordan, on the other hand, had been a saint. He spent most of the time playing in the sand or swinging. He tried to play with Tanner, but Tanner moved to the beat of his own drum.

Jordan nodded and climbed into the car and buckled himself in. Beth took a deep breath and pulled open the driver's door. After she was buckled, she started the engine and pulled away from the park.

Her stomach rumbled. Somehow, in the chaos of the day, they hadn't eaten lunch. Which meant, these two little boys were hungry. Wow. She was the worst nanny.

"Hungry?" she asked, glancing over her shoulder.

There was a cheer from the backseat. It wasn't the most nutritious, but Beth drove to McDonald's and ordered them each a Happy Meal. Once they were happily eating in the backseat, she headed back to Tricia's house.

When she pulled into Tricia's driveway, she took note of Josh's truck that was still in the driveway. He was still here. Excitement coursed through her veins until she saw her reflection in the rearview mirror. She looked crazed and sweaty.

She attempted to adjust her hair and dabbed at the makeup smears under her eyes.

Tanner and Jordan had already jumped from the car and were racing up to the door. Realizing that she was still on duty, she grabbed as much garbage as she could from the back and got out.

"Wait up, guys," she said as she rushed over to the garbage bin and dumped the lunch trash into before taking off after them. Just as she shut the door behind her, she backed up, running straight into a brick wall—at least what felt like a brick wall.

"Humph," she said, reaching out to steady herself. Instead of finding sheetrock, two hands wrapped around her arms, and a deep chuckle caused her stomach to lighten.

"Where are you off to in such a hurry?" Josh asked with a hint of teasing in his voice.

Beth glanced up at him, suddenly realizing how close they were standing. Desperate to maintain some mystery between them, Beth stepped back, breaking his hold on her. Right now, she was pretty sure she was as smelly as she was sweaty.

"Sorry," she said, tucking some of her hair behind her ear and peering up at him.

Josh studied her for a moment before his heartwarming half-smile emerged. "It's okay. I'm just happy I was here to save you." Then he winked. Again.

Beth nodded as she forced down the feelings that were bubbling up inside of her. Why was she so ridiculous to think that he could possibly like her? He hadn't done anything years ago, when they were kids, so the chances of him suddenly declaring his love for her were almost non-existent. She just needed to get that through her head and then she'd be fine.

"Thanks," she managed, glancing around. "Where are the boys?"

Josh studied her for a moment longer before glancing toward the living room. "They went through there. Tanner said something about dinosaurs, and Jordan was all ears."

"Oh, you're back," Tricia's voice cut up their conversation as she appeared next to them.

Beth couldn't help but notice how close they were standing to each other. Pushing that thought from her mind, she nodded at Tricia. "Yeah. Tanner is..." How could she put this delicately?

Tricia's face fell. "Oh, no. What did he do?" She moved toward the living room. "Tanner!"

This was the last thing Beth wanted, getting Tanner in trouble. He was just a spirited kid. Plus, maybe he needed some time to adjust to her. "I meant to say, sweet. Tanner is a sweet kid." Beth raised her hand, hoping to stop Tricia from getting upset.

Tricia pinched her lips together and studied Beth. Then a look of relief washed over her face. "Oh good." Then she crinkled her nose. "Isn't he the best?"

Well, best was probably pushing it. Spoiled would be how Beth would categorize him. But she figured that she shouldn't be calling the child she was nannying spoiled on the first day. "Yes," she said, nodding.

She glanced at Josh, who was watching her. Exhaustion took over, and suddenly she was ready to move on. "We didn't make it to the grocery store," she said, giving Josh a sheepish look.

Josh shrugged. "It's okay. Actually, I was going to see if I could catch a ride to the office? Dad said I could go finish getting things ready and spend some time with Jordan." A forlorn look passed over his face, and for a moment, Beth allowed herself to wonder what that meant.

The look passed just as quickly as it had come, making Beth wonder if she had even seen it.

Beth nodded. "Sure. I can do that."

"Great," he said.

"Wait. You're leaving?" Tricia asked, jutting out her bottom lip and stepping closer to Josh. Beth tried not to notice the way she ran her finger along his forearm.

"Yeah," Josh said, moving to slip his boots on.

"Can we do dinner sometime?" Tricia asked with a whiny hint to her voice.

Not wanting to stand there, listening to them make dinner plans, Beth excused herself and went off to look for Jordan. She passed a few empty rooms before she found Tanner's room. Both boys were sitting on the ground, playing with a heaping pile of dinosaurs.

"Hey, Jordan, we gotta go," Beth said, stepping into the room.

She could see the protest form on Jordan's lips but then it disappeared. "Bye, Tanner."

Tanner just grunted in response.

Beth said goodbye as well, but Tanner didn't acknowledge her. Instead, he continued setting up a line of dinosaurs, so Beth followed Jordan to the front door.

Josh was standing there with his hand on the doorknob. "Ready?" he asked.

Beth nodded, and they all followed him out to the driveway, where they climbed into her car and she pulled away.

SEVEN

JOSH

JOSH SAT in the front seat of Beth's car with his arms folded, frustration still coursing through his veins. He couldn't believe that his ex-wife had the nerve to call him up and ask him for visitation rights. What did he care that she was pregnant and wanted her kids to know each other? She'd been the one to leave Jordan. This wanting him back only when it was convenient wasn't okay.

"You okay?" Beth's soft voice broke his concentration.

He glanced over at her to see her soft smile. His heart quickened its pace as he studied the way her lips tipped up or the hinted dimple on her cheek. He let out his breath, and the tension in his chest lessened. He rubbed his hand on his thighs as he muscled down his anger. "Yeah. Sorry," he said.

Thankfully, Jimmy was pretty understanding, and had allowed Josh to take the rest of the day off. Right now, Josh needed to be with his son. Plus, he was feeling guilty that he had no food in his cupboards.

"You know, I'm a pretty good listener," Beth said, peeking over at him.

"I'm sure you are." He glanced behind him toward Jordan, who was sitting in the back, gazing out the window. "It's just not something I'm ready to talk about right now."

Beth nodded. "I get it. It's okay."

He couldn't help but notice that she looked sad. And for some strange reason, he had this strong desire to make her happy. "Maybe once I've worked through it, I'll share. I just..." He blew out his breath as frustration crushed his chest. "I need to figure out where I stand on the issue first."

"Of course. If there's anything I can do, let me know."

Josh studied her. It was comforting, knowing she was there. With Beth, things had never been super complicated. She was sweet, and drama didn't follow her like it did with his ex. He liked that.

"I do have one favor to ask," he said.

"Okay?"

"Come grocery shopping with me?"

Beth glanced over at him. "You want me to go get groceries with you?"

Josh nodded. "My mom may be a wiz in the kitchen, but that is not a gene she passed on to me. The extent of my cooking is boiling water to make ramen."

Beth chuckled as she pulled into the parking lot of

Braxton Construction and idled there. "I guess I can help you out." She smiled over at him.

He couldn't help the grin that emerged as he felt for the door handle. "Great. Let me clock out, and I'll grab my truck. Follow me to the Pick 'n Save?"

Beth smiled back at him. "Sure."

"Coming with me, buddy? Or staying with Ms. Beth?" Josh glanced back to his son.

"I wanna stay," Jordan said.

Wow. Ever since the divorce, Jordan had stuck to him like glue. The fact that he wanted someone other than Josh surprised him. And made him feel a bit grateful. Maybe this meant Jordan was healing from the mess he'd been dragged through.

Heaven knew they both needed to do that.

Beth gave him a small smile and shrugged as she nodded toward the back. "I guess the squirt is staying with me."

Josh chuckled as he pulled on the door handle and stepped out. "Guess so." He leaned down before shutting the door. "I'll be just a minute."

Beth nodded, and he shut the door. A warm feeling spread through his body as he crossed the parking lot and pulled open the door to the building. Tiffany was sitting at the desk with the phone pressed to her ear. She was typing fervently on the keyboard and muttering a few, mm-hmms.

Josh waved to her, and she acknowledged him with a flick of her head before she returned to her computer screen. Once Josh clocked out, he muttered a goodbye and stepped out into the late-afternoon heat. He was actually excited to be taking a break and getting things settled.

And doing those things with Beth helped buoy him up. He climbed into his truck and started the engine. After backing out of his spot, he nodded toward Beth, who smiled. He pulled out onto the main road and started down toward the Pick 'n Save.

Ten minutes later, he pulled into a parking spot. Just as he moved to jump from the cab of his truck, Beth pulled in next to him. He smiled as she climbed out of her car, followed by Jordan. They were talking about Spiderman, the superhero Jordan was obsessed with.

"That's amazing," Beth said, the smile on her lips drew Josh's attention.

He'd never realized it until now, but Beth had the sexiest lips. They were plump and red, with a perfect little Cupid's bow at the top. Suddenly, he realized that he was staring at Beth's mouth, so he dropped his gaze down to Jordan, who had his hands positioned like Spiderman and was making web-slinging noises.

"You get that kid talking about Spiderman, and you might never be able to get him to stop," Josh said as they walked through the sliding doors of the Pick 'n Save. The cool inside air surrounded them as Josh grabbed a shopping cart.

Jordan was too busy slinging his imaginary web to notice that Mrs. Corry, the mayor's wife, was trying to exit with her overflowing basket of groceries.

"Jordan," he scolded.

Mrs. Corry raised her hand as she shook her head. She was the same age as Josh's mom and had the same understanding look on her face. "Oh, please, I don't mind. Seems like the boy has a lot of bad guys to catch." She winked at Jordan and then pretended to release a few bits of web from her wrists as well.

Josh gave her a thankful smile as she passed by. But, instead of continuing to the parking lot, she paused, reaching out to grab Beth's hand.

"How are things?" she asked with her brow furrowed.

Beth's cheeks heated as she dropped Mrs. Corry's hand and grabbed her own arm in a protective movement. For a split second, she flicked her gaze over to Josh before returning it to Mrs. Corry.

"Fine. Things are fine." The laugh that escaped her lips sounded almost desperate.

Josh couldn't help but study her. Why was she acting so strange?

Mrs. Corry seemed to pick up on Beth's reaction. "Are you sure? Because I heard—"

"Yep, everything is fine. Thank you for asking. Now, you probably want to get that to your car before you ice cream melts." Beth nodded to both of them before disappearing into the grocery store and heading over to Jordan by the quarter toy machines.

Josh turned his attention back to Mrs. Corry, who

looked as confused as he felt. "What was that about?" he asked.

Mrs. Corry shook her head as she focused on the food in front of her. "Apparently a bit of gossip that wasn't true." She whispered in a way that made it sound like it was more for her than for Josh. He waited, to see if she was finished. She paused before bringing her gaze up to him and smiling. "Well, I should get going. It's good to have you back, Josh."

Josh smiled and muttered, "It's good to be back, too," and pushed his cart into the grocery store and over to Beth and Jordan.

"Ready?" he asked.

Whatever had been bugging Beth had passed. When she turned, her cheerful smile had returned. "Yes."

Josh felt more confused than ever, but didn't feel as if it were his place to pry. Instead, he hoisted his son up over his shoulder and pushed the cart one-handed into the aisles.

Jordan squealed and shrieked, drawing the attention of most of the people around them. Josh just gave them a smile and a nod and decided to ignore the judging looks some were shooting their way.

"Daddy, put me down," Jordan wailed.

Josh chuckled as he lowered Jordan to the ground. "It's the only way to get him away from those machines without a meltdown," he said to Beth, who looked amused. He couldn't help the teasing tone to his voice or the desire to lean in closer to her.

She was mysterious and familiar at the same time. He

liked that she was simple. A representation of a time in his life when things made sense. When he wasn't confused by a cheating ex-wife or a stubborn five-year-old. It helped calm him, and, right now, he needed the calm she brought.

"You're a good dad," she said, turning to the shelves and picking up a jar of grape jelly. "Does Jordan like this?"

He shook his head and leaned forward to grab the strawberry jam. He tried to ignore how good it felt to brush her arm with his own. Or the little zaps of electricity that raced up his skin.

That was an unexpected but not unpleasant reaction to Beth. She must have felt something to because her eyes widened, and she took a small step back, turning to return the jelly. A spark of satisfaction rose up inside of him when he realized he wasn't the only one feelings things.

"Strawberry jam. Got it. I'll remember that for the future."

Future. Wow. That word sounded good and scary at the same time. He liked the fact that Beth thought that way. That she thought she'd be around long enough to actually use that knowledge again.

"And we like crunchy peanut butter," Josh said, nodding down the aisle.

Beth glanced in the direction he motioned and nodded. "Crunchy," she said, pointing at the shelf where the crunchy peanut butter was.

"I can write it down if you want me to," Josh said with a wink.

Beth shot him a look. "I think I can remember that."

"I hope so." The smile that emerged on his lips was one he couldn't quite control. It had a flirty feel to it, even though he wasn't sure how to do that anymore. Maybe he should lay off. He didn't want to mess things up or creep her out.

But from the blush that showed up on her cheeks, maybe he wasn't as bad as he thought.

Jordan came barreling up to them with a box of Swiss Rolls in his hands. Josh glanced over at him as he chucked the box into the cart. "I want these," he said, his eyes wide and pleading.

Josh chuckled as two thoughts formed in his mind. He didn't like giving in to his son's every whim—it would make shopping with him unbearable—but he also knew that Jordan was going through some things too. If buying a box of Swiss Rolls made him happy, he'd do it.

"Sure, squirt," he said, reaching out to tousle Jordan's hair.

They made their way through the grocery store, grabbing food along the way. He kept the conversation light with Beth. He learned she had just come back a few weeks ago. That she was living with her mom and stepdad to help them out—she didn't say with what—and that her siblings were all keeping their distance. Apparently, there had been some drifting apart in their family.

There were a few times when Beth's voice sort of drifted off, like she was thinking about something, but not really saying what. Then, a few seconds later, she'd return to the present and glance over at Josh with a sheepish look and apologize.

Whatever was going on with her family, she was tight as a ship about it. As he leaned over the meat counter to pick out the pieces of steak for tonight's dinner, Josh couldn't help but wonder what was happening. Normally, he was a box of pasta kind of cook, but tonight felt special. Like the start of his new life without Cindy.

And he could do this. He had to do this. There was no way he was going to let his ex back into his life. She'd given up her parental rights. There was no judge anywhere that would force him to give her visitation.

He didn't have to give in to her ridiculous request. Just because she was pregnant, she wanted her son back? No. He wasn't going to do that to Jordan. It was his responsibility to protect his son, and that's what he would do.

"Everything okay?" Beth's soft voice broke through his thoughts.

Startled, Josh turned to see that she was inches away. Her eyes widened, and a worried look passed over her face. "I'm sorry. I don't mean to pry."

Feeling guilty that Beth thought his frustration was about her, he shook his head and reached out to gently take her elbow. When her gaze dropped down to his hand, he wondered for a moment if he'd made a mistake, but then he decided it was probably best to just own it.

"It's not you," he said, giving her arm a soft squeeze and

then dropping his hand. Out of instinct, he brushed his fingertips with his thumb as the memory of her skin against his own remained.

Beth cleared her throat. "Oh. Okay." She glanced toward the glass case full of meat and then back over to him. "If you ever want to talk, you know, I'm here."

Josh smiled and leaned toward Mr. Porter, who'd just stepped up to help them. After Josh told him the cuts of meat he wanted, Mr. Porter got started filling the order.

Now free, Josh turned to Beth. "I appreciate that. And when I'm ready to talk about it, I'll let you know."

Beth chewed her lip as she nodded. There was a look in her gaze that told him she understood. That she didn't need to know. That secrets were okay. It was refreshing, especially after living in a small town with his ex where everyone wanted to know exactly what was happening in his life.

Mr. Porter handed over the meat wrapped in brown packaging. Josh took it and turned to Beth. "Let's get the vegetables, and then I think we are ready to head home. Want to stay for dinner?"

She studied him. Did he really just ask her to come to dinner? Not really processing what it meant, she just nodded as she followed him to the casher.

After they paid, Josh wheeled the groceries out to his truck. After packing Jordan into the cab, he moved to the tailgate. After loading the bags inside, he slammed the tailgate shut and turned to see Beth studying her phone. Her expression had grown serious as she took in a deep breath and glanced over at him.

"I should go. I actually..." She took a deep breath. "Would it be terrible if I asked for a dinner raincheck? I have...something I need to do."

Josh tried to hide the disappointment he felt from her sudden change in plans, but he couldn't very well demand that she eat dinner with them. "Of course. Tomorrow?"

Beth gave him a small smile and then reached into the truck to tousle Jordan's hair. "Sounds like a plan."

When Beth stepped away from the cab, Jordan glanced up as if he suddenly realized that she wasn't coming. "Where are you going?" he asked, a sad hint to his voice.

Beth's face grew soft as she stepped back over to him. "I need to go home, buddy. But I promise, I'll be over tomorrow." She offered him a high-five which he was more than happy to return.

Once Jordan was settled back down, Josh shut Jordan's door, effectively giving them some privacy.

"I think he's smitten with you," Josh said, nodding toward his son.

Beth's cheeks flushed as she glanced over to Jordan's window. "He's a good kid." Then her expression grew serious as she studied him. "You've done a good job. You should be proud."

Josh peered over at her as her words washed over him. The feeling in his chest was hard to explain. It was like everything that he'd wanted to hear for so long was finally being said.

It was like Beth was telling him he could do this. And for some reason, with her confidence, he felt as if he just might be able to.

EIGHT

BETH

BETH PULLED into her driveway and let out a huge sigh as she shut off her engine. What was she doing? Why was she allowing herself to get involved with Josh? Did she think that her life had somehow worked out all the complications that had been created when Zander had walked out on her? That she was magically healed?

She squeezed the steering wheel as she leaned forward. No. If anything, Mom's illness had only made things more complicated. She was an idiot to think that anything could happen between her and Josh.

Plus, with Tricia circling him like a hungry vulture, Beth was a fool to try to get in the way.

She took a deep breath as she stepped out of her car and slammed the door. Out of instinct, her gaze made its way over to the Braxton house—more specifically, over to where

Josh had just gotten out of his truck as well. He was making his way to the tailgate. Then, as if he sensed her stare, he turned and waved in her direction.

Butterflies took flight in her stomach. She swallowed as she tucked her hair behind her ear and turned to make her way into her house. She was grateful for the break from Josh. It was easier not to think about him when he wasn't around.

After slipping into her house, she shut the door quietly and glanced toward the living room, where she expected her mom to be sitting in the armchair. But it was empty.

Panic rose up in her chest as she scanned the room, hoping that her mom was okay.

"Mom?" she called out when she saw nothing.

No one responded.

"Mom?" she called out again, this time more desperate. She began opening doors and checking all the rooms.

Nothing. Empty.

Her body was hot from adrenaline. What if her mom had gotten hurt? What if she was passed out somewhere? Just as she went to open the bathroom door of the master bathroom, she heard a moan.

"Mom?" she asked as relief flooded her body so fast that she began to shake.

"Beth?"

"Yeah, it's me," Beth said as she slipped between the door and the frame to find her mom lying next to the toilet.

She was pale and had her eyes shut. "What are you doing in the bathroom?"

Her mom moaned as Beth reached down to help her stand.

"I got sick, and I guess I fell asleep."

Beth slipped her mom's arm around her shoulders and helped her from the bathroom over to her bed. Her mom collapsed on the mattress. Once she was situated, Beth grabbed the comforter and pulled it over her lap.

"You should have called me," Beth scolded as she brushed her mom's hair back from her face.

Her mom shook her head. "I'm fine. Just, having a bad day." She opened her eyes as she studied Beth. "Call Sam?"

"Of course." Beth called her stepfather and, after a few minutes, hung up. "He's on his way home."

Her mom pushed both hands on the mattress as she attempted to sit up. After a few grimaces, she was sitting up with her back against the headboard. "Water?"

Beth nodded and, within a minute, returned with a glass in hand. After a few drinks, her mom started to look a bit better. "Thanks," she said, handing the glass back to Beth.

Beth set it on the nightstand next to her.

"How was your first day?"

Beth took the time to tell her mom about Josh not having groceries, about Tricia and Tanner, and about Josh inviting her over.

Her mom gave her a weak smile as she rested her hand

on Beth's. "I'm happy things are working out for you," she said.

Beth hated how weak her mom sounded. Such a stark contrast from the vivacious and lively woman Beth remembered, growing up. "But I can stay. I don't have to go to dinner."

Joanne shook her head. "No, of course not. You should go. I don't want to tip anyone off. It's best to keep up appearances." She squeezed Beth's hand. "You'll do this for me, right?"

Beth swallowed as she began to nod. Why did her mom even have to ask? She was tasked with keeping a secret, and she'd do just that. But the look in Joanne's eyes told her there was doubt lingering there.

"I promise," she whispered. Except she'd already told Josh she was busy. But her mom didn't need to know that. Besides, with the feelings that were surfacing about Josh, it was better if they spent the evening apart. Maybe Tiffany wasn't busy.

Joanne nodded and then sighed. "Thank you," she whispered.

The deep tones of her stepfather's voice carried into the bedroom. Beth called out, "We're in here." And moments later, he appeared in the doorway.

"What's going on?" he asked.

"Beth was just telling me about her day," Joanne said as she pushed herself up to a sitting position.

Beth studied her mom and parted her lips to correct her, but a desperate look told her to keep quiet.

"Everything okay?" he asked, a worried look passing over his face.

Joanne scoffed and nodded. "Of course. You worry too much."

No, her stepfather worried the perfect amount. It was her mother who thought that things were fine. Who didn't want to face the reality of her situation.

Sam studied Joanne before sighing. "I'll get started on dinner."

"Just for two. Beth's going over to Josh's."

Beth gave her stepdad a weary smile when he glanced over at her. She hated the amount of lies she was having to tell. Some to her mom, some to the town, and a whole lot to herself.

"Josh Braxton's?" Sam asked.

Beth nodded.

"Have fun."

Beth chewed her lip. She wanted to tell them that if they needed her, she'd stay, but neither seemed to even notice that she was still in the room. After she slipped out into the hall, she took a deep breath and glanced back to her mom's bedroom.

What was going on? Why were they pretending that things weren't as bad as they appeared? It frustrated her that she was the only one who seemed to realize the gravity of their situation.

She shook her head as she made her way into her bedroom and shut her door. After she changed into a soft satin top and a pair of hunter-green shorts, she pulled her hair up into a loose ponytail and slipped on her sandals.

She glanced in the mirror and winced. The day had really taken a toll on her. She looked as tired as she felt. After brushing on some foundation and lip gloss, she headed down the hall and out the front door.

Now alone on the stoop, she glanced down at her phone. It would be too telling if she got into her car just to go to the Braxton's, so she took off down the street. After locating her phone, she called Tiffany. She picked up on the second ring.

"Hello?"

"What are you doing right now?" Beth asked, taking note of the loud music in the background.

"I'm at the Tavern. Where are you?"

"Wanna come pick me up?" Beth asked, praying that Tiffany would say yes.

"Yes!" Tiffany said, a bit too enthusiastic.

Beth shook her head. Tiffany was definitely an easy-going, take life by the horns kind of gal. Something that Beth lacked in spades. Maybe that's why they were such good friends. They balanced each other out.

Beth gave Tiffany her location, and, ten minutes later, a pink VW bug pulled up beside her. Beth glanced over to see Tiffany in the backseat.

When she realized the ride was for her, Beth pulled open the back door and slipped onto the seat. "Who's this?"

she asked, nodding toward the particularly tanned man in the driver's seat.

"This is Juan, and he's delectable," Tiffany said, leaning over and wiggling her eyebrows.

Beth shook her head. Ever since high school, Tiffany had been a flirt. Always ending up on a new guy's arm every other week. Not much had changed in their adult years. It amazed Beth how easy being in a relationship was for Tiffany. If she were honest, it was something she envied about her friend. For Tiffany, love didn't come with a lot of stress like it did for Beth.

"Hello, Juan," Beth said, nodding toward the driver.

"Where to?" he asked in a spicy accent.

"The Tavern," Tiffany said.

Juan took off down the road, and Beth settled into her seat.

A few seconds later, Tiffany leaned into her and gave her a smile.

"So, how was your first day working for Josh?"

Beth took a deep breath as she thought back to Josh and their conversations. Of how easy it was to talk to him at the grocery store. Why did being around him feel as easy as breathing?

"It was good." She gave her best friend a relaxed smile. "Get this, I went to Tricia Young's house, and guess who's her new nanny?" Beth raised her eyebrows as she pointed to her chest.

"No. You?" Tiffany asked as she sat a little straighter so she could meet Beth's gaze.

Beth nodded. "Yep. I get to watch two kids now." She rubbed her temples as she thought about what she'd done. Was she really ready for this?

"Wow." Then Tiffany nodded. "You're nicer than me. But that's good. From what I hear, Marcus left Tricia a wreck." Tiffany patted Beth's hand. "You're a good person to help out."

Beth thought about explaining that Tricia was paying her a ton of money to help out, but figured she should keep that to herself.

They fell into a relaxed conversation about Tiffany and the trip that she just got back from. Beth laughed as the familiarity of hanging out with her best friend washed over her. It felt so good to be sitting here, where she didn't have to worry about her mom, or Zander, or her complete lack of direction.

Right now, it was about having fun, and she was ready for some fun.

It didn't take very long for Juan to pull into the Tavern's parking lot and announce that they had arrived. Tiffany flung some bills at Juan and climbed out. Beth thanked him as she climbed out as well.

When Tiffany rounded the hood, she linked arms with Beth.

"You know what you need?" Tiffany asked as she pulled Beth toward the front doors.

Beth laughed as she followed. "What?"

"We need to find you a date. How long have you been pining after Joshua Braxton?" Tiffany clicked her tongue as she raised her finger. "Don't answer because the only answer is *too long*."

Beth's stomach lightened at the thought of Josh and the feelings she'd harbored since she was a kid.

Her grandmother had always talked about that once in a lifetime, mind-changing love that weasels its way into your heart and doesn't let go. If she were honest with herself, that was how she felt about Josh. Even though she'd attempted to move on, her thoughts and feelings always came back to Josh. It was going to take some incredible guy to get her to move on.

So she patted Tiffany's hand that was hooked around her arm and just smiled. "Okay, Tiff," she said as she reached out and pulled open the door to the Tavern.

Loud music and the salty smell of pretzels and booze wafted out of the bar. Beth took a deep breath as she followed Tiffany inside. There were a few shouts of hello as they made their way deeper inside.

Beth waved at a few Honey Grove graduates as she made her way to the bar, where she leaned against the counter and waved down Freddy, the owner of the Tavern.

"Well if it isn't little Bethy Johnson," Freddy said as he grabbed a glass from the back and flipped it over. He held a nozzle to the rim. "What'll you be drinking?"

Beth shook her head. "Nothing alcoholic for me. How

about some Sprite?" The last thing she needed was to be wasted in case her mom needed her. It was best to keep all of her wits intact.

Freddy chuckled as he pressed a button, and bubbly Sprite filled the glass. "Sounds good."

Beth thanked him as she took the glass and turned. As she scanned the crowd, her heart dropped. The front doors had just opened, and guess who came walking in?

Josh.

NINE

JOSH

JOSH GLANCED around the crowd at the Tavern and sighed. What was he doing here? This wasn't his scene anymore. He was a dad. With a kid. That he'd left at home with his mom so he could go to a bar with his buddies.

Man, he felt like the worst dad.

"If it isn't Nerves of Steel," a loud voice boomed from the center of the room.

Just hearing his high school best friend's voice made Josh smile. He turned to see Spencer push through the crowd with his arms extended.

"I didn't believe that the prodigal son returned, but now that I see it..." Spencer dropped down to one knee and pressed his fist to his chest as he leaned forward—like he was a knight bowing to his king. "I will always be a believer."

Josh chuckled as he waved his friend up. "I release you," he said, mimicking Spencer's motion and bowing slightly.

Spencer stood and wrapped his arm around Josh's shoulders. "Let's get this man a drink," he yelled as he pushed Josh through the crowd and over to the bar.

Freddy already had two pints of beer ready for them.

"Freddy, my man," Spencer yelled as he grabbed a glass and held up the still-foaming liquid.

When Josh didn't move to take one, Spencer glanced over at him. "What's wrong? Your taste buds change since you moved to Colorado?"

Josh shook his head. "No, man. My responsibilities." He leaned over and motioned for Freddy. Once he'd ordered a root beer, he turned back to Spencer. "I've got a kid now."

Spencer sucked in his breath as a pained expression passed over his face. "Oh, that's right. I heard that somewhere."

From the way Spencer was talking, it sounded as if Josh had just confessed he had a boil. Like having a kid was the last thing a guy his age would want.

But, knowing that Spencer wouldn't understand, he just gave his friend a smile and settled back as Spencer talked about all of his business plans.

Apparently, Spencer had opened a gym in Honey Grove, and he was trying to motivate the town's residents to join.

Josh just smiled and nodded, enjoying the ease of spending time with his friend. And perhaps enjoying just being Josh, not Josh the dad and recent divorcé.

A blonde woman approached Spencer and linked arms

with him, drawing him out onto the dance floor. Spencer looked as if he wanted to resist, but Josh just laughed and waved his friend away.

Even if Josh wasn't interested in picking anyone up, he shouldn't stop his friend.

Now alone, he turned back to the bar and glanced around. At the other end of the bar, someone caught his attention. He squinted through the dark room at the familiar blonde hair and soft smile.

Beth.

A smile played on his lips as he pushed off the counter and made his way over to her. She was fiddling with a straw inside of what he could only guess was Sprite. She didn't notice him approach, so he reached out and brushed his fingers on her elbow.

"Hey," he said.

Beth jumped, knocking her straw from the glass and flinging her drink everywhere.

Feeling sheepish for startling her, Josh gave her an apologetic smile. "I'm so sorry. I didn't mean to freak you out."

Beth took a deep breath as her cheeks flushed. "Oh, no. That's okay." She grabbed a few napkins from the dispenser in front of her and mopped up the spill. Then she turned and gave him a smile. "Hey."

Taking her acknowledgment as an invitation, Josh sat down on the stool next to her. He set his root beer on the bar and grabbed a few pretzels. When she didn't speak, he glanced over at her.

"So was going to the Tavern the thing you needed to do?" He leaned closer to her so he didn't have to shout over the music that was blaring from the speakers.

Beth glanced over at him, and it wasn't until her lips tipped up that he realized just how close he really was. In an effort not to freak her out, he pulled back a smidge so she didn't feel like he was invading her space.

"I, um..." She glanced back at the bar.

"It's okay. I mean, I'm not the greatest cook. Freddy, now, he's a cook." He waved his hand in Freddy's direction.

Beth laughed as she glanced up to where Josh motioned. Then, when she dropped her eyes to meet his gaze, her expression turned sheepish. "I had to take care of a few things at home, and then Tiffany invited me out with her. I haven't seen her in forever." She reached out and ran her fingers along the rim of her glass.

Josh understood the feeling exactly. "It's different, huh?"

She glanced over at him. "What?"

"Being home after so long." He glanced around the crowd of people. Some he recognized. Some he didn't. "It's like you move away, and, while you're gone, you think your hometown just stops. That it will be the same when you come back." He took a long drink of his root beer. He glanced over at Beth, who had a contemplative look.

"But it seems as if life went on without you," Beth said. "And you struggle to know where you fit in a place that was your past but is now your future." Her voice was low as she stared off into the distance.

Josh nodded. He couldn't have said it any better himself. "Makes you wonder how to start your life again."

Beth laughed, but it sounded pained, like she saw the truth in what he'd said. "Yeah."

They sat in silence for a moment before Josh glanced over at her. "Wanna play darts?"

Beth finished her drink and nodded. "Sure."

He signaled a refill for the two of them as he pushed off the stool. Beth was already down and pushing her hair behind her ear.

"I promise, no more deep conversation," he said.

Beth laughed, and this time, it was much more light-hearted. She mimicked pushing up her sleeves. "Deal. But I have to warn you, I've gotten a lot better since the ninth-grade fundraiser."

Josh grabbed the full glasses and followed her over to the back of the bar, where the dart boards were set up. One was being used by a wobbly older gentleman, but the other was free.

"Oh, you mean when you skewered me?" Josh asked as he set the glasses down and made his way over to the board to grab the darts.

Beth's mouth hung open as she stared at him. "I did not skewer you."

Josh held her darts hostage while he waited for her to look at him. "Um, yes you did. I have the scars to prove it."

He pulled up his sleeve to expose his shoulder. Then he searched until he found the tiny dot her dart made years ago. "Right here."

Beth squinted and leaned in as if she didn't see it. "Where?"

Josh moved his arm so he could get a better view. There was a small, pink dot on his arm. "Right there."

Beth brushed her fingers across his skin, and warmth rushed through his body. He swallowed from the sudden touch. He glanced over at her, and thankfully, she didn't look as shocked as he felt.

"I'm not seeing anything." She glanced up at him and paused. Her sky blue eyes were wide as she held his gaze. "But I'm sorry."

Suddenly he felt like an idiot to harp on this. Josh just shrugged as he pulled his sleeve down and handed the darts to her. "It's no biggie. I survived. I found a very effective support group to help me get through it."

Desperate to lessen the tension that had surrounded them, he winked as he turned to the dart board. "Now, who wants to go first?"

Beth waved him forward. "After you."

Josh focused on the bullseye and raised the dart. He slowly released his breath as he let the dart fly. And just as he predicted, it soared through the air and hit dead center on the bullseye.

"Score!" he shouted as he raised his arms in triumph.

Beth scoffed. "Beginners luck."

Josh shrugged as he moved out of her way. She got ready to throw the dart but then paused, turning to face him.

"What if we made this interesting?"

Josh raised his eyebrows. "What do you have in mind?"

Beth chewed her lip. "For every bullseye I get, you have to tell me something about you that I don't know—and nothing about imaginary dart scars. And for every bullseye you get, I have to tell you something."

Josh scoffed as he studied her. "Are you sure you can handle it?"

Her cheeks hinted pink as a look of worry passed over her face, but then she brushed it off. "Would I offer it if I couldn't handle it?"

Josh leaned on the wall as he watched her. "Okay. I'm game if you are."

Beth nodded. "Perfect." Then she motioned to his bullseye. "We'll call that one your practice shot."

"Right." Then he coughed while muttering, "Cheater," under his breath.

Beth dropped her jaw as she turned to face him. "What did you call me?"

Josh faked an innocent look. "I didn't say anything."

Beth narrowed her eyes and raised her finger to him. "Yes you did. All right, I'll honor the bullseye. Ask me a question."

Josh studied her for a moment before he straightened and rubbed his hands together. "Here we go. What happened to the guy you were dating in Pittsburgh?"

Beth's expression faltered and Josh instantly regretted asking her. Even though his motives were purely innocent, he couldn't help but feel like he'd just dredged up a memory that Beth might not want to relive.

"I'm sorry, you don't have to answer."

Beth shook her head as she held up her hand. "No. It's okay. I made up the rules." She took a deep breath as she studied the darts in her hands. "I, um, he dumped me. Told me that I wasn't marriage material." She glanced up and gave him a weak smile. "Great, huh? Eight years in a relationship and he dumps me flat."

Josh flexed his jaw as he thought about the tool she had been dating. Who would say that to anyone, much less Beth? "He's an idiot," Josh said, letting his feelings reflect in his voice.

Beth glanced up at him and held his gaze for a moment before she turned to the board and readied her dart. "Maybe he was right," she said as she let go and the dart flew straight into the center circle.

Josh wanted to continue talking about this jerk and telling her that it wasn't true. That he was an idiot to treat her that way, but Beth looked like she'd moved on.

She turned back to him with a wide smile. "My turn."

Josh winced as he held up his hands. "Okay, but be nice to me."

Beth shook her head. "That wasn't the deal." She got a contemplative look on her face before another smile emerged. "I've got it."

Josh gave her a weak smile. "Let's hear it."

"At the festival the summer we both went to Camp Littleton, were you or were you not the one who put a snake in my bed?" She rested her hands on her hips as she stared over at him.

A laugh escaped his lips as he studied her. "Seriously? That was so many years ago."

"Yes, and because of it, I'm terrified of snakes." She waggled her finger at him. "So? Fess up. No lies."

Josh studied her and then raised his hands. "Okay, okay. Yes, it was me. I did it."

She clapped her hands. "I knew it. You were so mean."

Josh reached out and grabbed her clasped hands, the need to justify himself taking over. "But wait, you have to hear the reason why."

Beth's laughter died as her gaze made its way down to their hands. Suddenly, Josh realized that he was still holding onto her and that they were standing inches apart.

He dropped his hands and stepped back. "I'm, um, I'm sorry," he said as he pushed his hands through his hair.

A look he couldn't quite read passed over her face, but as quickly as it came, it disappeared. "It's okay," she said as she tucked her hair behind her ear. "I should probably go find Tiffany. I'm sure she's looking for me."

"Do you want to finish the game?" Josh asked. If he were honest with himself, he didn't want her to leave. He liked having her around.

Beth shrugged. "I came with her. I should probably find her."

Josh nodded as he fiddled with the darts still in his hand. "No, I get it. I can't monopolize your time. I mean, I'm already employing you."

Beth chuckled as she handed the darts over. "Right." Then she glanced up and met his gaze. "I'll see you tomorrow?"

Josh smiled. "Tomorrow."

Beth gave him one last smile before turning and disappearing into the crowd. Josh returned to the dart board and finished his game. After he let the last one soar—straight into a bullseye, he smiled and downed his root beer.

He couldn't help but replay his conversation with Beth. The relaxed feeling he felt while he was around her lingered in the air of this busy establishment. He'd enjoyed being around her. Well, maybe enjoyed was a bit too mild. Perhaps he was a little more excited than he let on.

For the first time in a long time, he just felt happy. And nothing was going to change that for him.

TEN

BETH

BETH ARRIVED at Josh's apartment at exactly eight the next morning. She stood outside the door and knocked. After waiting a few minutes, the door opened and Jordan was on the other side, staring up at her. One look, and he broke out into a smile.

"Ms. Beth," he said, stepping out onto the stairs to give her a hug.

Beth bent down and wrapped her arms around him. "Hey, buddy. Long time no see," she said as she tousled his hair.

Jordan sprinted back into the living room and plopped down in front of the television. Beth chuckled as she walked in and shut the door behind her. That seemed about right. Jordan's attention span lasted all of five seconds before he was onto something different.

Once she was inside of Josh's apartment, she slipped off

her shoes and padded into the kitchen. From the lack of dishes in the sink, she figured that no one in this house had eaten breakfast. She located two bowls and the Reese's Puffs that they'd bought during yesterday's excursion to the store.

"Hungry?" Beth called out, mostly to Jordan.

"Starving." Josh's playful response startled her.

She jumped and turned to find him walking into the kitchen with a smile on his lips. He looked just as good as he had yesterday at the Tavern. She was pretty sure he'd flirted with her last night, and if she were honest with herself, she'd flirted back.

She couldn't help the smile that played on her lips. "Good morning," she said as she turned back to the bowls and busied herself with pouring cereal.

"Morning to you too," Josh said as he reached around her to open a drawer.

Beth tried not to obsess about how close he was or that his arm had brushed her hip. But the tingles that raced across her skin were hard to ignore. Beth cleared her throat and grabbed the milk.

After the cereal was ready, she turned to search for the spoons only to find Josh standing behind her, holding them up into the air. "Looking for these?" he asked.

A flush rushed across her skin as she nodded and took them from him. She plopped a spoon in each bowl and took a step back.

"Come on, JP. Breakfast is ready," Josh shouted toward the living room as he grabbed the coffee pot from its base and poured a mug. "Coffee?" Josh asked, holding out the cup.

Beth nodded and took it from him. Josh poured another mug and then settled down at the table.

"So, how are you feeling?" he asked as he took a big bite of his cereal.

Jordan wandered into the kitchen and over to the table, and Beth brought him over his bowl of cereal. He seemed too distracted by the action figures on the table to notice their conversation.

Beth eyed Josh. "I'm okay." Why was he asking her how she felt? Did she look sick?

Josh shrugged and took another bite. After swallowing, he glanced over at her. "I just figured you might be sore from last night. I mean, since I walloped you at darts and all." He gave her a wink as he took another bite.

Beth's jaw dropped. "You did not wallop me."

Josh narrowed his eyes like he was thinking hard. "Yeah, I'm pretty sure that's what happened."

Beth scoffed. "Yeah, if you're delusional."

Josh chuckled and Beth couldn't help but smile. Why did things have to be so easy with Josh? Why couldn't he have changed into a horrible, ugly monster? It would be easier to deny her feelings for him if he weren't so...adorable.

A ringtone halted their conversation. Josh held up his finger as he grabbed his phone from his pocket. From the way his expression dropped, Beth could tell he wasn't happy with who was calling.

But, before she could ask, Josh stood and mumbled something about needing to take the call outside.

It wasn't her place to know his business, so Beth just gave him an encouraging smile as he walked over to the small door that lead out to the balcony. She tried to ignore how the air had shifted from relaxed to tense. And she tried to ignore the curiosity that built up inside of her as she wondered who would get him this upset.

Beth busied herself with finishing her coffee and rinsing out the mug. By the time she was finished, Jordan brought his bowl over and handed it to her. She took her time washing it, drying it, and putting it away.

A few minutes later, Josh came back in with a disgruntled look on his face. He pushed his hands through his hair as he blew out his breath and glanced over at the door.

"I should go. I'm going to be late if I don't leave."

Beth chewed her lip as she watched him walk over to his boots and slip them on. She wanted to ask if he was okay, but she also didn't want to pry. So she just nodded and said, "Of course."

Once Josh was ready, he made his way over to Jordan and plopped a kiss on the top of his head. "Mind Ms. Beth, you hear?"

Jordan mumbled something which Beth couldn't make out, but from the satisfied look on Josh's face, he must have complied. Josh walked by her, pausing briefly. "I'll see you at Tricia's?" he asked, glancing over at her.

Beth just nodded as she tried to muscle down the butterflies that had taken flight in her stomach. "Yes."

Josh met her gaze, and she could tell he was hurting. Whatever had transpired over the phone had hurt him. She wanted to reach out and comfort him, to tell him that it was going to be okay, but she didn't. Instead she just gave him an encouraging smile.

Josh turned and made his way out the front door. Seconds later, Beth was standing there in his house, alone. Well, except for Jordan. But he seemed completely content with sitting in front of the TV.

Beth turned and made her way over to the couch. "Come on, buddy. We have to go get Tanner."

Jordan grumbled something, but after a few more encouraging words from Beth, he stood and disappeared into his room to get dressed.

HEAT PRICKED Beth's back as she climbed into the driver's seat late that afternoon. She'd decided to take Jordan and Tanner to the beach, and what started out as a fun, adventurous afternoon excursion had turned disastrous.

After swimming out to get the floaties that both boys had let go of and brushing the sand off their sandwiches that had fallen to the ground, Beth was exhausted. She was ready to get home and shower to get the salt and sand off her skin.

After pulling out of the parking lot and heading down

the main road, Beth glanced behind her to see that both boys had fallen asleep. Grateful for some calm, Beth turned on the radio and settled back into her seat.

Half an hour passed before she was pulling into Tricia's driveway. Her gaze automatically made its way over to the black truck with the words *Braxton Construction* across it. After she turned off the car, she opened the door and stretched. She reached up and adjusted her messy bun, hoping she looked adorably disheveled instead of like a crazy sea creature.

Just as she went to wake up the boys, Josh's voice filled the air, making her shiver.

"Busy day?" he asked with an amused hint to his voice.

Beth straightened and turned to see him standing behind her. He was covered in dust and sweat, but with his playful smile and chiseled jaw, he'd never looked better.

Hoping that he didn't catch her staring, she shrugged and blew out her breath. "These two definitely keep me on my toes."

Josh reached out and rested his hand on the door—right next to Beth's. They were almost touching. Then he leaned down to peer into the car. "Looks like you did your job well. They look totally worn out."

Beth pulled her hand away and crossed her arms. Sure, Josh was intoxicating with his smiles and flirting, but she needed to be careful. This would not end well if she read too much into what he was doing. Besides, with her mom's illness and her relationship baggage, she was the last person Josh should be involving himself with.

"I'm happy I'm doing well," she said.

Josh glanced over at her, and then his eyebrows shot up as if he suddenly realized what he'd said. "I didn't mean—"

Beth held up her hand. "It's okay. I'm a novice when it comes to kids."

The smile that played on Josh's lips caused her heart to quicken. He straightened, bringing his entire frame upward to tower over her. "Well, from what I can see, you're a natural."

Beth stood there, dwarfed by Josh and completely unable to form any sort of coherent response. He was complimenting her, and that was strange. Worried she'd sound like an idiot if she opened her mouth, Beth just nodded.

"You're back," Tricia called out from behind Beth, breaking the trance Josh held over her.

Beth jumped back and whipped around to see Tricia peering into the car. "Yeah, sorry."

Tricia's eyes were wide as she brought her gaze up to meet Beth's. "Don't apologize. You wore him out. That's great." She made her way around the car so she could open Tanner's door. "This kid never gets exhausted." Tricia smiled at Beth. "You're a genius. Thanks so much for helping me out."

Beth nodded, and, as Tricia emerged with Tanner passed out on her shoulder, she turned to face Josh. "Think about it, okay? I think the boys would really enjoy a weekend away."

Beth studied Tricia and then let her gaze travel over to Josh. He was just nodding. Beth tried to keep her expression relaxed as she met Josh's gaze. But she must have furrowed her brow because Josh sighed.

"She wants to take the boys to Disney World next weekend."

Beth swallowed as she reached down to unbuckle Jordan and heave him up onto her shoulder. "Oh yeah?"

Josh nodded. "I'm just not sure that's a good idea." Josh led her over to his truck, where she deposited Jordan into his booster seat.

She brushed her hands as she turned to face Josh. "I think Jordan would have a lot of fun." She forced a hopeful smile as she met his gaze.

"Yeah, he would." Josh's voice drifted off as he stood there with one arm propped up on the cab of his truck and a far-off look in his eye.

Not sure what else to say, Beth took a deep breath and turned. "I should go. I'm covered in sand and salt." Just as she started her retreat, Josh's hand reached out and grabbed her arm. Heat raced across her skin as she glanced down to see that she hadn't been imagining the contact.

"Come to dinner?" he asked. His voice was low and husky and sent shivers down her back.

When she glanced up to see that he was inches from her face, all she could do was nod. "Sure."

That seemed to satisfy Josh. He gave her a wide smile and dropped his arm, allowing for Beth's hasty retreat. Once she was in her car, she started the engine and pulled out of Tricia's driveway, her heart pounding in her chest.

Why was she going to Josh's for dinner? Was she crazy? Probably.

AFTER BETH WAS SHOWERED and dressed, she left a quick note for her mom and headed out the door. As she walked by the Braxton's house, she could hear loud music playing from the inside. Elvis, Mrs. Braxton's favorite artist. Shadows moved past the kitchen window, and as she studied them, she realized that Mr. and Mrs. Braxton were dancing.

A smile played on her lips as she dropped her gaze, feeling like she was intruding on an intimate moment. But she couldn't stop the twinge of jealousy that grew in her gut. It'd been a long time since she'd seen her mom and Sam happy.

It was one of the things she missed most—before the divorce or even after. It'd been a long time since she'd seen a parental figure in her life laugh or dance together. But that seemed ridiculous given her family's circumstance. It hurt when she thought of all the things that her mom had had to give up, and she just wished she had more time to fix the broken things in her mom's life. Their relationship, her mom's happiness. Those things felt unreachable to Beth, no matter how hard she strained to reach them.

Tears pricked her eyes as she thought about the outcome that so many with cancer faced. What was she going to do without her mom? There were so many life experiences that she wanted her to be there for, and facing them alone felt daunting. And suddenly, she felt selfish. Here she was, allowing herself to be happy. To reach out to Josh, who seemed to be reaching back.

How could she possibly be happy when her mom and Sam were so unhappy? What kind of daughter did that?

She swallowed the lump in her throat as she forced those thoughts from her mind. She couldn't think like that right now. Not when she was moments away from talking to Josh. The last thing she needed to do was to break down in front of him. She was determined to keep her mom's secret. She could do this.

She patted her cheeks and took a deep breath, willing her tears to dissipate. Just as she reached up to knock, the door opened. She was met with Josh's wide eyes and equally wide smile.

"Hey, you made it," he said as he pushed some shoes away with his foot and opened the door wider. "I was about to send up a smoke signal."

Beth shook her head and smiled as she stepped into the room. "Sorry. I had to take a shower and leave my mom and Sam a note."

Josh nodded as he shut the door behind her. "Good. I

was worried they were upset that I keep taking their daughter away from them." He gave her a wink.

Beth knew that he meant it in jest, but her heart picked up speed from his words. As much as she wanted to deny it, Josh clearly wanted her here. And that felt so good.

Deciding that it was better not to focus on his meanings or non-meanings, she slipped her sandals off and stepped into the living room, where Jordan was doing a puzzle.

"Beth," he said, jumping up from the floor and rushing over to give her a hug.

"Hey, Jordan," she said as she wrapped her arms around him. She loved the fact that he was happy to see her. It felt good to be greeted with enthusiasm instead of the cloud of worry that hung over her house.

"I'm working on a puzzle," he said as he grabbed her hand and pulled her toward the coffee table.

"Wow, that looks amazing," she said, staring down at the half-finished puzzle.

"Want to help me?"

"Hey, squirt, I need Beth to help me with dinner," Josh said as he appeared in the doorway to the kitchen.

Beth glanced up at him, and heat rushed to her cheeks. He was leaning on the doorframe, watching them in an unabashed and open way. Even though her whole body was responding to the way he was looking at her, fear crept up into her chest, causing her to drop his gaze and shrug at Jordan.

"Is that okay with you?" she asked.

Jordan shrugged as he attempted to shove a puzzle piece into place. He wasn't heartbroken that she wasn't going to stay, so Beth stood and made her way over to Josh.

He didn't move as she stopped inches in front of him. "You need my help?" she asked, praying that her voice would come out normal.

Josh chuckled and pushed off the wall. He extended his hand into the kitchen. "If you don't mind."

She shrugged and tried to act as if his presence wasn't sending her senses haywire. Cooking with Josh by her side was like a dream come true. "I guess."

The steaks were laid out on the counter and coated in a spice rub. The potatoes were washed and stacked next to a bowl with a peeler resting next to them.

"Mind helping me with the potatoes?" he asked, picking one up and tossing it into the air.

Beth chuckled as she reached out and grabbed one from the top. "You're in luck. I'm the fastest potato peeler this side of the Mississippi." She turned her voice gravelly so she sounded like a pirate.

Josh's eyebrows went up. "Oh, then I am lucky. Wanna race?"

Beth settled down on one of the barstools and grabbed the peeler. "Oh, it's on."

Josh grabbed another stool and dragged it over so that he was facing her. After rummaging around in the drawers, he found a knife and raised his hands, poised to get started.

"Let's do this."

After he shouted, "Start!" they began peeling. Beth stared at the potato as she ran the peeler across the skin, shards of potato skin flying to the counter below. Just as the last strip was off and the potato was clean, she dropped it onto the counter and raised her hands.

"Done," she shouted and glanced over at Josh, who was still slicing the last of the skin off his potato.

He groaned as he finished and set his potato next to hers. "I demand a rematch."

Beth smiled smugly at him as she pretended to brush something off her shoulder. "Are you sure? I mean"—she sucked in her breath between her teeth—"I did beat you pretty badly."

Josh dropped his jaw. "Wow. Humility run in your family?"

Beth laughed. It felt so good to just goof off with Josh. There was no pressure here. Just the two of them and Jordan. It wasn't stressful. And she needed this so badly.

She shrugged. "Bring it on, sparky." She grabbed another potato and readied the peeler.

Josh chuckled. "Go."

They started peeling. Beth watched as the chunks of peel flew to the counter.

"Crap," Josh's voice pulled her from the trance she was in. Glancing over, she saw him grab his finger and squeeze.

Realizing what he'd done, Beth dropped her potato and peeler and rushed over to grab a paper towel.

"I'm so sorry," she said, her voice barely a whisper as she handed it over.

Josh took it, and as he unwound his fingers, she could see the blood covering both hands.

"Why are you apologizing," he said. "It was my own dumb fault. I got sloppy."

Beth still felt terrible. Josh dipped down to meet her gaze.

"It wasn't your fault." His smile was soft and genuine as he studied her.

"Let me help you clean it up," she said as she waved to his hands.

He paused but then nodded. "Sure."

Beth glanced up to meet his gaze. He had a soft smile on his lips. She tried to control her emotions. "First aid kit?" she asked.

Josh stood and nodded for her to follow. Beth glanced into the living room as they passed, to see that Jordan had given up on his puzzle and was now watching a superhero show.

As Josh lead her down the hallway and into his bedroom, her heart began to pound in her chest. This situation was beginning to turn intimate, and as her mind swam from that thought, panic rose up in her chest.

Opening herself up to Josh was the last thing she needed to do. But from the way he stood close to her in this tiny bathroom, it was going to be near impossible to avoid.

ELEVEN

JOSH

JOSH COULDN'T HELP but stare at Beth as she gingerly took his hand and brought it over to the running water. Her expression stilled as she glanced over at him.

"I'm sorry," she said as she tipped his hand to and fro. Blood mixed with the water and ran down the drain.

Josh wanted to tell her that he'd been injured worse than this in the past, but he kind of liked how gentle she was being. It'd been a long time since someone cared about him enough to dote on him.

"I'm sure I'll be fine," he said. He shifted on the toilet seat so that his arm wasn't bent in a strange angle.

"I'm such a dork. We shouldn't have raced when knives are involved." She shot him a sheepish look. "I mean, I am supposed to be a good example now that I'm the nanny."

Josh laughed and leaned in. She smelled like coconut

and vanilla. He could breathe in her scent all day. "I won't tell your boss," he said, making it sound as devious as possible.

It may have been his imagination, but he swore he saw goosebumps rush across Beth's skin. He wanted to study it more, but she dropped down to grab his first aid kit from under the sink. When she returned, she looked completely normal. As if his words hadn't affected her.

He felt stupid. Why was he seeing things that weren't there? Even though things were changing for him, it didn't mean they were changing for Beth.

He dropped his gaze and focused on what she was doing. Zaps of electricity raced up his arm as she carefully lifted his hand up to inspect the cut. Warmth flooded his chest as she gently dabbed his finger with gauze to remove the blood that welled from his cut.

"You should be a nurse," he said.

Beth snorted and glanced over at him. "I'm okay with a little blood, but pools of it make me woozy."

Josh chuckled as she dabbed the blood again and then grabbed the antiseptic cream and squeezed a line down his cut. She wrapped a bandage around it and then crumpled up the trash. Josh reached out his hand to take it from her, and for a moment, she looked startled.

"Garbage is over here," he said, nodding toward the wastebasket next to him.

Beth's face flushed as she nodded and dropped it into his

hand. She was confusing him so much. There were moments when he wondered if she liked him, and then she would back away as if she were afraid of something.

He understood what it was like to be hurt. To build a wall up around your heart so that no one could ever hurt you again. But that wasn't him—he would never hurt her. And all he wanted to do was prove that to her. But how?

Beth began rinsing the sink with water as the last of the blood flowed down the drain. Josh took the job of collecting the cream and box of bandages and returning them under the sink.

He stood and suddenly realized how small this bathroom was. As he remained there, looking down at Beth, his mind began to swim. All he could focus on was how good it felt to be this close to her.

She knew him, and that thought comforted him. They'd grown up together. She was as familiar as breathing.

Time seemed to stop as he dropped his gaze down to study her. She met it with so much uncertainty that Josh almost found himself telling her that she could trust him. That hurting someone he'd known for so long was the last thing he'd do.

"How does your hand feel?" she asked, her voice low and breathy.

Josh reveled in the fact that she hadn't stepped back or tried to leave. Did he dare think that she wanted to stay? Was that crazy?

"Much better, thanks to you," he said, the depth of his voice surprising even him.

She flicked her gaze down to his hand and then back up to him. "I'm happy to help."

Out of instinct, Josh reached up to tuck a loose strand of hair behind her ear. His heart raced as his fingers brushed her smooth skin, and the desire to touch more raced through him. "I'm happy I came home. It's been nice having you around." He met her gaze. He wanted her to know that he meant what he was saying.

Beth chewed her lip as she studied him, but before she said anything, the sound of a phone ringing caused her to jump back.

"That's my phone," she said as she stepped out of the bathroom.

Josh watched her disappear around the corner. He took a deep breath as he ran his thumb over his fingertips. The memory of how it felt to touch her was burned in his mind and on his skin.

She was no longer that little teenage girl who had declared her love for him. Now they were older, and it changed everything. She was kind and sweet and everything his ex wasn't. And he was ready for different. If only she felt the same way.

THEY FINISHED up dinner with pleasant conversation. Jordan dominated most of it, talking about superheroes and the beach. Beth seemed entertained by everything he said, giving him her undivided attention.

Josh just sat back, enjoying how Jordan lapped up her enthusiasm. It'd been a long time since anyone had paid that much attention to his son. Cindy had always found reasons not to engage with him.

Once their plates were empty, Josh brought them into the kitchen and rinsed them off. When he returned to the table, he saw that Jordan had dragged out his coloring books and laid them in front of Beth.

They began coloring and talking about which superhero could kick another superhero's butt. Josh enjoyed listening to their voices and laughter as he cleared the table. There was a knock on the door just as he started the dishwasher.

Intrigued, Josh headed to the door, but Jordan beat him to it.

"Nana," Jordan exclaimed as he threw his arms around Sondra's middle.

"Looks like you have a full house here," she said, glancing first at Beth and then appreciatively to Josh.

Josh squelched the desire to roll his eyes as he shot his mom a look. "I invited Beth over for dinner. She worked hard today."

Sondra gave him a *sure you did* look before turning her attention back to Jordan. "Grandma just pulled out some chocolate chip cookies. Want to come over for some?"

Jordan cheered and rushed to slip on his flip-flops. When Josh moved toward the door, Sondra held up her hand. "Invitation is for grandchildren only."

Josh shot her a hurt look, but she held her ground. "Besides, you have company." Sondra nodded at Beth.

He sighed, but she just chuckled under her breath as she held the door open for Jordan. "I will return him in an hour."

Josh waved at his son as they descended the stairs and then shut the door. Realizing how alone they were, Josh glanced back to see that Beth had stood up and looked as if she didn't know where to go.

"Wine?" he asked as he grabbed two glasses and a bottle from the fridge.

Beth's eyes widened as her gaze flicked over to the door. Josh tried to not let that bother him. Maybe she really did need to leave. Maybe he'd misread every signal he thought she was sending his direction.

She had a crush on him when they were kids, but maybe she'd moved on a long time ago. He was a fool for entertaining thoughts of something more.

"I mean, if you have the time. If not, I totally understand." He began to open the fridge to return the wine.

Beth shook her head. "No. That's okay." She took a deep breath. "I'd love to have a glass."

Josh's confidence returned as he nodded toward the sliding doors that lead out to the small balcony. The nice thing about South Carolina was that, while the sun was blazing hot during the day, the nights were cool.

Beth walked over to the doors and pulled them open. Josh followed after her, and just before he passed by, he paused, reveling in the feeling of standing next to her.

He leaned closer, hoping she would understand his meaning without saying it. "I'm really happy you decided to stay."

Beth met his gaze, and for a moment, it was just the two of them. All he could see was her. He loved the familiarity that he felt, being next to her. It was strange to think, but even though he'd spent most of his teenage years ignoring her, he was grateful she was here right now.

She swallowed and nodded. "Of course. What are friends for."

Josh cleared his throat at her choice of words. *Friends.* Even though it felt like a punch to the gut, he didn't allow it to shake his resolve. He knew what she was doing—it was something he was all too familiar with.

Protection. That's what she was giving herself. A fire lit inside of him as they settled into the deck chairs out on the balcony. He loved a good competition, and Beth had just extended one.

This was a competition for him to prove how he felt about her, and he was up to the challenge.

Once they were situated and the wine poured, Josh settled back in his chair. He took a drink and then set his glass down on the little table between them.

The salty smell of the ocean wafted with the breeze. He took a deep breath. This was amazing. He didn't realize it until now, but he'd missed this. All of it.

He glanced over to Beth, suddenly wanting to know everything about her. Everything that had happened over the last fourteen years since he'd seen her. But he didn't want to push her farther then she wanted to go.

"It's good to be home," he said, smiling over at her.

Beth glanced at him while taking another sip. She nodded, pinching her lips together as she swallowed. "It is. There's no place like Honey Grove."

Josh snorted. "That's for sure. Colorado was nice, but I missed this place. This town. The people." He let his last words linger in the air as he studied her.

Did she understand his meaning? Honestly, he didn't even understand his own meaning. He didn't want to lead her on, though he did want to connect with her. Could he be that kind of guy for Beth? He wasn't sure. He just knew he wanted to.

Beth's cheeks flushed, telling him she'd understood. "Your family is great. I missed them too."

Josh's gaze turned toward his parent's house. Lights shone through the windows and against the ground below. He had missed his family. Life wasn't the same since he left. He'd gone from a house full of people and love to a house with Cindy.

He just wished someday Jordan would feel the love that he'd felt growing up in a town like Honey Grove.

"Poor Jordan," he said. Pain clung to his throat, making the words almost impossible to get out. He swallowed, trying to push down all the pain that had built up in his chest, but it didn't want to budge.

A hand curled around his own. Heat and electricity rushed across his skin from the contact. Glancing up, he saw Beth studying him.

"You're a good dad. Jordan knows that."

Josh cleared his throat as he turned his hand over, hoping that Beth would understand what he wanted. He didn't want this friendship between them. He wanted something more. How would she feel about that?

When she didn't move her hand away, he threaded his fingers through hers. "It's nice, being back with you." He gave her a small smile.

She returned it. "Yeah."

Hoping she would open up to him, he decided to try and to get her talking. "Your ex is an idiot."

A sad expression passed over her face, and Josh cursed himself. Why did he bring that guy up again? She probably didn't want to talk about it.

And when she pulled her hand away to adjust her ponytail, he knew he'd crossed a line. He should have kept his mouth shut.

"What do you mean?" She reached out to pick up her wine glass and hold it in her hand.

"I'm sorry. I shouldn't have blurted that out, but it's true. If that guy dumped you, he should be checked in to an insane asylum." Well, the truth was out. It needed to be said, but from the way his chest was constricting, he worried he'd said too much.

Beth started at him as if she weren't sure how to answer him. Then she sighed and brought her knees up, balancing her glass on them. "I'm not so sure, but that's okay. It's good that he dumped me instead of dragging things out longer. Now, we can both move on."

Josh nodded as he turned to watch the last bits of orange sunlight disappear beneath the horizon. He knew that all too well. How much of his life did he give to Cindy, just to have her rip it out from under him.

"Cindy, my ex, decided that my business partner was more interesting than me." He swallowed as a lump formed in his throat. It wasn't from sadness, more from frustration at himself for being so stupid. He should have seen this coming, but he'd just ignored it.

When Beth didn't respond, he continued. "She decided that she needed a fresh start with him. And Jordan and I weren't included. So she gave up custody and walked away." He reached out and downed the rest of his wine in one gulp. Wow. That hurt to even say.

Which made him feel ridiculous. How long had it been since this happened? Why was it still hitting him like it was fresh?

He was stronger than this. He was stronger than his cheating ex-wife.

"I'm so sorry, Josh. She was a fool." Beth's voice was soft and soothing. And he loved it.

Glancing over at her, the desire to kiss her took over. Her lips were soft and supple, and her spirit was sweet and gentle. Everything Cindy wasn't.

He swallowed as he allowed his gaze to linger on her lips. He didn't even care if she noticed. And when he met her gaze, he saw something there. A desire that filled his chest.

She wanted him too.

He set down his glass on the table and stood. Throwing caution to the wind, he reached out and grabbed her hand. A soft tug, and she was standing—inches from his chest.

He could feel her heavy breathing as he wrapped his arm around her waist and drew her in close.

"Josh," she whispered.

When he glanced down at her, he saw her eyes were wide and there was a hint of fear in them. She was worried, and that was the last thing he wanted her to feel.

"Beth," he said, cradling her cheek against his palm. "I don't know how..." He let his words drift off as he debated what to say. Just as he gathered his strength to be truthful with her, a phone rang.

It was coming from Beth.

Her eyes widened as she reached behind her and pulled it out. One glance at the screen made her face drop. In a matter of moments, she pulled away.

"I—I've got to go," she said.

Before Josh could respond, she was gone, and he was standing on his balcony alone and confused. Worried that he'd just made a giant mistake.

TWELVE

BETH

BETH GROANED as her alarm sounded the next morning. She flung her arm over her eyes as she attempted to block out the world.

Just when she thought she and Josh would have their moment, her phone rang. Sam. Mom wouldn't stop throwing up, so Beth had rushed home to help load her up into the car and take her to St. Jude's in Jordan, an hour away. It have been a long night, but the doctors eventually calmed Mom's stomach down, and she was going to be there for the next 24 hours for observation.

It wasn't until two in the morning that Beth finally crawled into bed and fell asleep.

Her alarm sounded again. It didn't seem to care how stressed she was, it had a job to do. Groaning, she pulled the blankets off her lap and stumbled into the bathroom, where she showered and dried off.

She threw on a white shirt and jean shorts, slipped on her Converses, and threw her hair up into a messy bun. With the way she felt, today was a casual day.

After a quick bowl of cereal, Beth slipped out of the house. There was no way she wanted to stay in that place a moment longer. Everything reminded her of how sick her mom was.

The sun was peeking up over the horizon as she crossed the street and made her way up the Braxtons' driveway. The sky was streaked with purples and yellows.

She climbed the garage stairs two at a time, and when she got to the top, she knocked.

When no one responded, she turned to handle to discover that it was unlocked. Quietly, she pushed it open, half expecting Jordan to be on the couch, watching TV. But there was no one there. She entered and slipped off her shoes.

The apartment was eerily quiet as she glanced around. Not wanting to just stand there, she made her way into the kitchen and located the peanut butter and jam from their grocery shopping trip and set them on the counter.

Might as well get lunch covered right now. She wasn't sure what was happening with Jordan and Tanner, so she figured being prepared was the smartest option.

"Jordan, what are you doing?" Josh's voice grew louder.

Beth tensed as she closed her eyes. The memory of their almost-kiss the night before washed over her. What had she been thinking? There was no way she was ready for any of that. Not with Zander's words still lingering in her mind or with her mother lying in a hospital bed.

She was a fool to think that anything could happen between them.

"Beth, you're early," Josh's voice sounded from behind her.

Gathering her strength, she turned and almost dropped the butter knife. Josh was standing in the kitchen with just a towel wrapped around his waist. His hair was damp, and drops of water still clung to his shoulders, chest, and...

"Yeah...I..." Words weren't forming in her mind. All she could think about was his muscular chest and toned abs. Instead she just nodded as she unscrewed the peanut butter cap and dipped the knife into it.

The tension between them was thick. Beth could probably cut it with the knife she was holding.

"Sorry. I thought Jordan was getting into things. I'll go get dressed," he mumbled as he backed up toward the hallway.

Beth nodded, keeping her gaze trained on the sandwich bread. He turned and left. Once he was gone, she let out the breath she'd been holding.

Wow. Time had certainly been good to Josh. How was she supposed to stay away from him when he wandered around the house in a towel? Next time, she was not coming in until she was certain everyone was up and dressed.

There was no way she could keep her resolve if she saw him half-dressed on a regular basis.

Once the sandwiches were made, she packed them in a black cooler she'd found under the sink and continued collecting lunch items from the kitchen. By the time she was zipping the top closed, Josh came back into the kitchen, this time dressed in dark jeans and a black t-shirt.

He had a concerned expression when he met her gaze.

Worry brewed inside of her, and she stepped toward him. "What's wrong?"

Josh cleared his throat as he walked over to the kitchen counter and flipped on the coffee maker. "Jordan's not feeling too good. He's...kind of warm." He took down a mug from the cupboard above him and set it down on the counter.

"Okay, what can I do?" A protective feeling clung to her chest as she thought about that little boy. Even though it had been only days since she met him, she couldn't help but care for him. Much like she was rapidly doing for his father.

"Just keep him here and monitor him." Josh scoffed as he ran his hand through his hair. "Squirt didn't even want to get out of bed. That's how you know it's bad." He sighed as he pulled the coffee pot from the base and poured himself a cup.

After a few sips, he set his mug down and glanced over at Beth. She must have looked worried because his furrowed brow relaxed.

"Don't worry, Beth. I'm sure he'll be fine. Kids get fevers all the time. We just need to monitor it."

Even though Josh was trying to help her feel better, it

wasn't really working. Not when every pet her parents had given, her had met an untimely death. She didn't need a repeat of her gecko or hamster.

"Are you sure? Do you think I'm the most qualified to stay here?" She studied her hand as she listed off ten people in her mind, all of which would be better equipped than her to keep Jordan alive and well.

Suddenly, Josh appeared in front of her. His hand reached out and cradled her elbow. "It's just a fever, Beth. I'm sure he'll be fine."

Warmth spread across her skin from his touch. She couldn't help but glance down and study his hand. Was it wrong that her heart was pounding in her chest? She didn't want him to stop touching her. In fact, her body longed from him to touch her more.

But she knew nothing could happen between them. Her life was a mess, and her mom was forcing her to keep a giant secret. One that she wasn't sure how to keep quiet anymore.

So, despite the fact that she wanted to lean into his touch, she moved her arm slowly away, to brush her hair from her face.

If Josh noticed, he didn't say anything. Instead, he folded his arms across his chest as he studied her.

Beth let out her breath as the stress that had built up inside of her diminished. "Okay. Just keep your phone on you in case I need to get a hold of you."

Josh traced a cross over his heart. "You have my word."

Beth nodded, and, as she glanced around the room, she suddenly felt foolish for having packed the cooler. "If you want some lunch, I made some."

Josh glanced behind him, toward the lunch box. "Great. Thanks."

Not wanting to stand there and stare at Josh as he got ready for the morning, Beth grabbed her phone from her pocket and held it up. "I should let Tricia know I won't be there today." She didn't wait for him to respond. Instead, she headed into the living room and dialed Tricia's number.

It took some convincing, but Beth finally got Tricia to calm down and realize that bringing Tanner to Josh's house, where he could get sick as well, was probably not the smartest idea.

By the time Beth hung up, Josh had his boots on and the lunch box slung over his shoulder. He waved to Beth as he pulled open the door. Just before he shut it, he told her that he would call to check in during his lunch break.

Grateful to have some space away from Josh so that she could actually think about her feelings and what they meant, Beth returned his wave and gave him a relaxed smile. Even though she was a jumble of nerves inside, she forced herself to be calm.

She could do this. She could take care of Jordan. Besides, she had experience taking care of her mom. How was this any different?

BY MIDAFTERNOON, Beth's worry was on full alert. She'd checked on Jordan a few times, feeling his forehead and waking him up to make sure that he got some fluids. But, each time she went into his room, he was more lethargic than the last.

After digging around in the bathroom cabinet, Beth finally located the thermometer and took his temperature. 103.4 degrees.

Panic rose up inside her chest as she reached out and felt his forehead for what seemed like the hundredth time today. Why wasn't it getting better? She'd given him a fever reducer, but it didn't seem to be working.

Jordan moaned as he tried to lift up his arm. His eyes fluttered open, and instead of being bright and full of excitement, his gaze was dull and cloudy.

"How are you feeling?" she asked, but then felt stupid. Of course he felt terrible.

"Mommy?" Jordan glanced over to her. It took a few seconds, but recognition passed across his face. "Ms. Beth," he said as he collapsed on his pillow. "Where's Daddy?"

Her heart broke that this poor, sick kid was stuck with her, instead of his parents. She reached out and rubbed his arm—something she'd beg her mom to do growing up. Jordan's expression relaxed, and it didn't take long before he was asleep.

This was one of the few times in Beth's life that she felt completely helpless. Most of the other times had to do with her mom. It was excruciating to sit back and watch someone you love be in pain. If she could, she would take it all away. For her mom, and for Jordan.

Frustrated, she slipped out of Jordan's room, shutting the door behind her. She shouldn't be here. Josh should.

Walking out to the kitchen, she located her phone and called Josh. After listening to the ringtone over and over again only to end in his voicemail, she let out a frustrated groan. She took a deep breath to try and calm her nerves, and she hung up and tried again. Why wasn't he picking up? He'd promised.

After trying to reach him a dozen times more, she finally set her phone down on the counter. What was she going to do? Jordan seemed to be getting worse, not better.

Tricia. She could try her. She picked up her phone and called the only number she had. A ring barely sounded before three beeps and an annoying voice filled her ear. "I'm sorry, but the number you are trying to reach is currently out of order. Please hang up and try again."

She let out a groan as she tried the number again only to have the same thing happen.

Panic rose up. How could it not be working? She'd used this same number to contact Tricia just this morning. The feeling of helplessness rushed through her, and she started shaking. She located Mrs. Braxton's number and tried that. Finally, after three rings, she picked up.

"Hello?"

"Mrs. Braxton?"

"Beth? Honey? What's wrong?"

"I, um, I'm watching Jordan, and his temperature keeps rising, and nothing I do seems to be working. Josh told me to call him, but he's not answering, and I don't know what to do." Her words rushed out of her mouth like a strong summer breeze.

Mrs. Braxton was quiet for a moment. "Honey, I'm about an hour away visiting my mom. Pack him up and take him to the Emergency room. It's better to be safe than sorry. He's probably dehydrated, and they can give him an IV."

Beth nodded as she located a notepad and pen. For some reason, she needed the security that writing down Mrs. Braxton's words gave her. She cared about Jordan and didn't want to see anything happen to him.

"Okay," she breathed out, feeling rejuvenated.

"I've got five minutes left here, and then I can head out."

"Right." Beth was already over to the door and slipping her shoes on. She was nodding even though she knew that Mrs. Braxton couldn't see her.

"I'll keep calling Josh. You just worry about Jordan."

"Thank you." She grabbed her purse and slung it over her shoulder. After she said goodbye to Mrs. Braxton, she quietly went into Jordan's room and slipped her arms under his knees and around his back. She lifted him off the bed, and, after grabbing a blanket to lay over him, she carried him from the room.

It amazed her how much strength she mustered as she

carried Jordan down the stairs and across the street and set him gently into the car. It must be similar to what people talked about when they said moms found the strength to lift cars off of their kids. Right now, she didn't care how much her arms burned or her legs shook. She was going to take care of Jordan even if it killed her.

THIRTEEN

JOSH

JOSH SWITCHED off the jackhammer and shook out his hands. He'd been working for three hours straight, and his hands were numb.

He rubbed his hands on his thighs and squinted as he glanced around. Tricia could be seen in the distance, talking to some guy in a dark blue jumpsuit. She looked pretty upset as she waved her hands in the air.

He leaned over and grabbed the glass of ice water that Tricia had her maid bring out to him. The ice clinked against the sides of the glass as he tipped it to his lips. The cool liquid rushed down his parched throat.

Man, he'd gone soft living in Colorado. This heat was definitely getting to him.

As he set his glass down, he noticed the screen of his phone light up. Anxiety pinged his chest as he picked it up. Was it Beth?

He clicked on his screen to see that he had a dozen missed calls from her and an equal amount from his mom. In his attempt to distract himself with work, he'd completely forgot about Jordan.

Wow. Dad of the year over here.

Just as he moved to pull up Beth's number, his mom's name flashed across the screen. He tapped the green button and brought the phone to his ear.

"Mom? What's going on?"

"Josh!" his mother exclaimed. "Where on God's green earth have you been?"

"Is it Jordan?"

"Beth took Jordan to the hospital. She couldn't get his temperature down. She's been trying to call you all day. I'm a half an hour out."

Josh was only half listening to his mom. He was already out of the pool and halfway across the yard. His dad was lingering by the truck, which was a miracle. It meant Josh didn't have to track him down.

"I've gotta take the truck, Dad," he said, lifting his hand.

Out of instinct, Jimmy threw him the keys without a word.

"Jordan's in the hospital. Fever."

Jimmy nodded. "Need me to come?"

"Mom will be there. I'll keep you posted."

Jimmy saluted him and stepped back as Josh peeled out of the driveway. The fifteen-minute drive to the hospital felt as if it took an eternity. Josh kept his hands grasped so hard on the wheel that his knuckles were turning white.

He took a few deep breaths as he lingered at a stoplight, but it did little for his nerves. By the time he pulled into the parking lot, he was more nervous than he'd felt in a long time. He had no idea what he would do if something happened to Jordan. It was his responsibility to take care of his son. How could he have failed him so horribly?

He pushed his hand through his hair as he walked through the sliding doors and made his way straight over to the woman behind the counter. She was talking on the phone, and it took all of Josh's strength not to reach over and hang up for her. She just acknowledged him with a raised pointer finger.

Finally, she hung up and turned her attention over to him. "How can I help you?"

"I need to see my son. My nanny brought him here." He let out his breath slowly so that it stifled his irritation. He doubted he would get anywhere with a curt tone.

The woman clicked on the keyboard for a moment before turning her attention back to him. "Son's name?"

"Jordan Braxton."

The woman typed that in and then studied the screen for what felt like ages.

"Josh?"

Beth's soft, nervous voice eased his frustration. He turned to see her standing next to him.

"Where's Jordan?" His winced at the bite in his tone.

He hadn't meant for it to come out like that, but he was on edge and nothing would calm him down until he saw his son.

"Follow me," she said, waving him toward the two wood doors to the right. She pressed the button on the left, and the doors swung open.

There may have been people lingering around as they walked past the beds, but Josh didn't notice them. All he focused on was finding Jordan. Finally, at the end, Beth pushed a fabric curtain open, and Josh laid eyes on his son. The relief that flooded his body almost caused him to shake.

Jordan looked pale, but his blue eyes were open, and he was sipping on a juice box with an IV hooked up to his arm.

"Daddy," Jordan said as he grinned over at Josh.

Josh dropped onto the side of the bed and pushed Jordan's hair back from his forehead. He allowed his fingers to linger on Jordan's skin, testing his temperature. "How are you feeling, buddy?"

Jordan gave him a huge, toothless smile. "Better." He leaned in toward Josh. "They give me all the juice boxes I want."

Josh smiled as he leaned in and kissed Jordan on the forehead. Jordan settled back against the pillows that were propping him up and continued sipping on the juice box until it was empty.

"I'll go get him another one," Beth said.

Josh suddenly realized that she was in the room. He glanced over at her just as she slipped through the curtains.

He couldn't see her face, but from the way her shoulders curved forward, he could tell she was stressed.

He glanced over at Jordan, who was fiddling with the buttons on the railing of his bed. "Hey, bud, I need to go talk to Ms. Beth. Do you think you'll be okay?" He shifted so that he could pull his phone from his back pocket. "Here, watch a show until I get back."

Jordan let out a whoop as he grabbed Josh's phone and selected a superhero cartoon. Surprise, surprise.

Satisfied that his son wasn't going to just get up and run off, Josh walked over to the opening in the curtains. Glancing out, he saw Beth on the other side of the room. She was crouching down in front of a small fridge. She grabbed a juice box and stood back up, keeping her eyes down as she walked back in his direction.

He didn't want to have this conversation in front of Jordan, so Josh slipped through the curtains and made his way over to her. Just before he reached her, a nurse walked between them, pausing to address Beth.

He couldn't quite make out what they were saying— their voices were low—but he could tell from their expressions that the nurse knew her. And when the nurse reached out to touch Beth's arm, Josh realized that the nurse was comforting her.

Why?

Beth nodded, and her conversation with the nurse ended. Beth gave her a smile and continued walking, this time, meeting Josh's gaze. A worried expression flashed over

Beth's face as she flicked her gaze from the nurse then back to Josh.

"Hey," she said as a smile spread across her face.

Josh studied her. That was a quick change of emotions. He couldn't help but wonder if her sudden smile was more forced than genuine.

He stepped closer to her, only to have her step back. He studied her, wondering what that had been about, but then decided to push that thought from his mind. He was here for Jordan, and Beth's strange reactions weren't what he needed to focus on.

"Thanks for doing this," he said as he shoved his hands into his front pockets.

Her smile faltered as she glanced behind him. She sighed as she fiddled with the juice box in her hands. "I'm so sorry. I tried to call you, but you didn't answer. He wasn't getting better. I...didn't know what to do." The last words left her lips as a whisper.

Josh could see the worry that she was holding onto. It made him both respect and care for her that much more. She worried about his son. Someone like that would always have a place with him.

"Well, you took good care of him, so thanks."

Beth continued to fiddle with the juice box for a few moments longer before she sighed and nodded toward Jordan. "I should get him this."

Josh wanted to stop her. He wanted to make sure she realized how grateful he was that she took such great care of his son. Even though he'd been saying the words, he wasn't sure she'd understood him. She was pulling back, and he wasn't sure why.

But he was determined to find out.

A doctor distracted him when he got back to Jordan, which helped keep his mind off of Beth, who was sitting in a chair next to Jordan's bed. The doctor said that Jordan was fighting off a cold, which most likely caused the spike in temperature which led to the dehydration. He said that after the IV bag was empty, Jordan could go home.

Grateful that it wasn't anything too serious, Josh shook the doctor's hand and thanked him. After checking a few more vitals, the doctor left them alone.

Jordan was focused in on the show he was watching while sipping the last of the juice, so Josh allowed his gaze to make its way over to Beth. She had her purse on her lap and was studying her phone. Josh wanted to open his mouth, to say something. But things were so strange between them. Ever since last night when he'd wanted to lean down and kiss her, things had changed.

"Excuse me, Mr. Braxton, but there is a Tricia here to see you," a nurse said as she poked her head between the curtains and glanced down at him.

Josh furrowed his brow, and from the corner of his eye, he saw Beth raise her head to watch them.

"Um, yeah, you can let her back here." What was he supposed to say? It wasn't like Beth was speaking to him.

Maybe having someone else here would help with the awkwardness between them.

It didn't take long before Josh could hear Tricia's voice as she made her way back. She was talking a mile a minute. When the curtains parted, the nurse looked all too happy to dump Tricia on them.

"Josh," Tricia exclaimed as she made her way over and threw her arms around him.

Josh stood there for a moment, almost shocked by the fact that Tricia was hugging him. Not wanting to be rude, he wrapped his arms around her and patted her back. "Hey, Tricia."

Tricia pulled back and met his gaze, but didn't let him go. "How's Jordan?"

Josh glanced over at his son and, in the process, caught Beth's eye. He couldn't quite read her expression. Was she happy? Mad?

Tricia ran her hands down his shoulders to his biceps and let her hands linger there. "I'm just shocked that you left without telling me. I mean, imagine my surprise when suddenly you were gone. You dad told me that you'd been called to the hospital. I left Tanner with the maid and rushed right over." She threw her arms around him again and hung onto him like he was about to float away. "I just didn't want you to be alone," she whispered loudly in his ear.

Josh gave her a quick squeeze and then backed away. "Well, I'm not alone. Beth is here."

A look of hurt flashed over Tricia's face when Josh stepped back, but it was quickly replaced with a huge smile that seemed a little forced. "Beth is here. Of course." She turned and located Beth. "You were so smart bringing Jordan here. A temperature is nothing to mess with."

Beth had tucked her phone back into her purse and nodded. "I wanted to make sure he was okay." She stood and reached over to give Jordan a quick hug and kiss on the top of his head. "I should probably go. I need to get back. Since you're here, I figured you can take over."

Josh parted his lips. He wanted to ask her to stay. There was no reason she should go. He liked having her here. But Beth just gave him a quick nod and slipped from the makeshift room.

Once Beth was gone, a new life came over Tricia. She turned and grinned at him.

"Well, you have me now, and I'm not leaving until he's discharged." Then she leaned in, brushing her shoulder against his. "And maybe not even then."

Tricia held to her word for the next hour and a half. Apparently, a few serious cases came in to be treated, halting all the discharges. By the time they walked through the doors that evening, Josh was cranky and so was Jordan.

Tricia didn't seem fazed at all. She was happy to just talk, even though Josh had stopped responding. There was a moment where Tricia brushed her hand against his and it made him wonder if she wanted him to hold it. Then he dispelled that thought as fast as he could.

Cindy had done a number on him. He used to be a confident guy. In high school, if he wanted a girl, he went after her. Now? He couldn't read Beth, much less Tricia. Maybe this whole thinking about dating thing had been a colossal mistake.

He was pretty sure he was misreading everything, and if he wasn't careful, he'd not only end up alone romantically, but he'd ruin all his friendships. So he made sure to move away from Tricia. Maybe she'd get the hint that he just wasn't interested right now.

His life was a mess. Jordan was sick, and he still hadn't figured out what he was going to do about his ex. Trying to involve himself with anyone romantically was a stupid idea.

He just needed to get that through his head before he saw Beth again. Before his resolve completely crumbled down around him.

FOURTEEN

BETH

BETH STUDIED the road as she drove back home from the hospital. So many emotions were rushing around inside of her as she took a deep breath and pressed on the brake, pausing at an intersection before taking a left.

What an emotionally charged day. First, she'd been worried about Jordan and had to make sure he was okay. Then she'd been worried about what Josh would say when he came. And then there was Tricia—a factor she hadn't prepared herself for.

They had seemed so intimate when Tricia greeted him, and their hug had thrown Beth off. Was there something there?

She groaned as she pulled in to her driveway and rested her forehead on the steering wheel. Of course there was something there. It was Tricia. Perfect, rich, and incredibly single, Tricia.

Josh would be an idiot not to like her.

Beth sighed as she pulled on her door handle and got out. Right now, she needed a hot shower and her comfy pajamas. She unlocked the front door and made her way into her house. It was eerily quiet.

Sam had texted her to tell her that they were staying an extra night at the hospital but not to worry, that they would be home soon and things could return to normal. But Beth knew how to read between the lines.

This secret was getting ridiculous. Almost detrimental to her mom's health. Plus, she was exhausted from keeping it to herself. Keeping it from Josh.

She climbed the stairs to her bedroom and set her stuff down on her bed. After a long shower, she emerged from the bathroom with her fluffy robe wrapped around her and her hair pulled up in a towel.

As she walked into her room, she let out a scream.

"Tiffany," she said, grabbing her chest as her heart pounded.

Tiffany had a confused expression as she turned, holding Beth's phone up. It took a moment for everything to register for Beth. Tiffany looked worried and was holding her phone. What had she found out?

"What are you doing?" Beth asked, crossing the room and grabbing her phone from Tiffany.

"Why is Sam texting you about how someone has cancer?" Tiffany asked as she collapsed on Beth's bed.

Beth gave her an annoyed look as she slipped her phone into her robe's pocket. "The cat."

Tiffany didn't look convinced. "Really? Beth, come on. Why are you lying to me?"

Beth sighed as she sat down on the armchair in the corner of the room and cradled her forehead in her hand. "Tiff, I can't..." Her voice trailed off as all the emotions she'd been trying to suppress came bubbling up. Well, there was no way she could convince Tiffany that there wasn't anything going on, now. Her dumb emotions were giving her away.

Tiffany's feet appeared on the carpet in front of her, and then her hand rested on Beth's shoulder. "Beth, what's going on? Is it your mom?"

Beth took a deep breath as she nodded into her hand. "She's sick. Has been for a while." Beth straightened as she brought her gaze over to the picture hanging on the wall. Anything to avoid the pity that was coming from Tiffany. So this was why her parents wanted to keep it a secret. Now she knew.

"Beth, I'm so sorry. Why didn't you tell me?"

Beth brought her gaze over to Tiffany and attempted a small smile. "She made me promise not to say anything, and, you know, I couldn't break that promise. Not when she's sick and our relationship is what it is."

Tiffany sat criss-crossed on the carpet. "Yeah, I get that."

Beth pinched her lips together. Her life was a complete mess. What was she doing? Either with Josh or with trying to attempt to have a normal life. It was ridiculous. That was never going to happen.

"Is there anything I can do to help?" Tiffany asked. "I came over, hoping we could go out. It is a Friday night. But..." Tiffany raised her eyebrows.

Beth shook her head. Honestly, she was exhausted. "I just want to be alone if that's okay."

Tiffany furrowed her brow but then nodded. "Of course." She stood and straightened her clothes. "Tomorrow? Let's do something."

Beth nodded as she wrapped her arms around her chest. She wasn't going to think that far into the future. Right now, she just needed to get through the night. Tiffany gave her a hug and left, the click of the door marking her departure. Beth lingered in the chair until she gathered the strength to stand.

After slipping into her pajamas, she pulled the towel off and began running a comb through her hair. Just as she finished the braid, her phone rang.

She got up and made her way over to her purse.

Josh.

Worry rushed through her as she clicked the phone on and raised it to her ear. "Hello?"

There was a pause. "Beth? It's Josh."

She nodded. She already knew that. "Hey."

"Hey."

Silence.

This was a strange phone call.

"I just wanted to thank you again for what you did for Jordan. He hasn't stopped talking about you since we left the hospital."

Beth's heart swelled. She really was falling for that kid. "I'm just happy he's safe."

"Yeah. Had a hard time going down for bed, but I finally got him asleep."

Beth glanced out her window toward the Braxton's garage. She could only imagine which window Josh was standing behind. Was he thinking about her like she was thinking about him?

No. That was a stupid thought. He should be thinking about Tricia. She was much less complicated than Beth.

"How did things go with Tricia?" Then she pinched her lips together. Why did she ask that? Did she really want to know his answer?

There was a pause. Beth could literally hear her heart beating in her ears from the anticipation of what he was going to say.

"She stayed a bit longer once you left but then had to get back to Tanner."

So she wasn't over at his apartment. That was good news.

"Oh." She wasn't sure what she was supposed to say.

"I'm not only calling to thank you. I was wondering if you wanted to come over. I just..." He let out his breath as his voice deepened.

He sounded stressed. And beaten down. Like he needed

a friend. She could be that friend. "Sure. I can come over. I'll be there in a few." If anything, that would probably be better for Beth. Staying alone in a house full of memories was the last thing she wanted to do. And after her conversation with Tiffany, the reality of her future never felt more certain.

Josh mumbled a thank you, and Beth hung up the phone. After slipping into some shorts and a t-shirt, she grabbed her sandals, slipped her phone into her back pocket, and left.

She tried to slow her gait as she crossed the driveway and climbed the stairs to the apartment. After one knock, the door sung open and Josh's weak smile greeted her.

"Hey," he said, backing away from the door to let her in.

She tried to ignore how close he remained as she stood in the entryway to take off her sandals. She tried to ignore how good he smelled or the burning desire she had to wrap her arms around him and take away all the hurt that was written on his face.

Once she straightened, she met his gaze. He held it for a moment longer than a friend would, and suddenly, Beth's heart took off in a gallop. She wasn't just seeing things. Or hoping.

Josh was treating her differently, and it wasn't just her imagination.

Taking a chance, she reached out and touched his elbow. Too nervous to find out how he felt about her attempt to comfort him, she studied her hand.

"What's going on?" she asked. She glanced up to see that he was staring down at her. There was an intensity to his gaze that caused her breath to hitch in her throat.

He stepped forward, and everything around Beth seemed to fade away. All that mattered in this moment was the two of them. Her feelings for him crashed through her body like waves against the shore. It made her lightheaded and woozy.

He lingered for a moment longer before he turned toward the kitchen. "Chocolate milk?" he asked.

Just as he moved away, reality fell down around her. This was his moment to show her how he felt. To open up to her, and yet, he wasn't. What did that mean?

Feeling like an idiot, she wrapped an arm around her stomach and held onto her other arm. She needed the protection that brought. How could she have allowed herself to think that Josh would see her as anything other than the little girl from across the street who confessed her love for him?

"Um, sure." She followed after him, keeping her distance. There was no way she wanted to get into a situation like that again. She didn't want to allow herself to feel vulnerable around a guy just to have him back away.

Josh nodded as he got two glasses down from the cupboard and set them on the counter. Then he grabbed the milk from the fridge and poured it.

"Can you grab the chocolate powder?" he asked, motioning toward the cupboard just behind her.

Beth nodded and stepped back, pulling the door open and glancing inside. After locating the powder, she set it on the counter. Josh grabbed a spoon and Beth opened the lid. After scooping the powder into the milk, Josh handed her the spoon. Just as she grabbed it, her fingers grazed his.

Zaps of electricity rushed up her arm. Beth scolded herself for reacting that way. What was the matter with her?

Josh didn't seem to notice. Instead, he reached into the drawer and grabbed another spoon. After stirring his milk a few times, he drank half of it.

Not sure what to do, Beth did the same. Why weren't they talking? Did he literally just invite her over for chocolate milk? That seemed strange.

After finishing off his drink, he made his way to the sink and set his glass inside of it. Beth held hers in her hand, feeling awkward. Where was this night going?

"Thanks for the milk," she said, holding up the glass.

Josh glanced over at her and nodded. "Of course."

She sipped on it as she glanced around. What was the matter with her? Why couldn't she be as smooth and put together as Tricia? She hadn't realized it until now, but Zander had pulverized her confidence. Even though she had never been a naturally outgoing person, she'd still been confident. Now, she felt as if she were hanging on to everything around her by a fraying thread.

Who was she fooling? Josh was smooth and handsome. He seemed like he knew exactly what he wanted. Why would he ever look at her?

"I should probably go," she whispered as she walked over to the sink and set her glass down next to it.

"Cindy wants back into our lives." Josh's words caused her to stop. She glanced over at him. He'd dropped his head and his shoulders slumped.

"What?"

He tipped his head over to her and gave her a weak smile. "She wants Jordan back. Apparently, she's pregnant and wants Jordan to know his brother." He reached up and rubbed his face with his hand.

Beth wasn't sure what to say. Did that mean they were going to get back together? "How do you feel about that?"

Josh sighed, his shoulders moving up and down. "I don't know. I'm just not sure if I can let her back into my life. She's toxic. But she's Jordan's mom. How do I keep him from his mom?"

Beth chewed her lip as she thought about what he was asking. Truth is, she wasn't sure how anyone handled that. At least with Zander, she could just walk away. She didn't need to interact with him all the time. With Jordan keeping them connected, Cindy was someone Josh was never going to be able to shake.

"I wish I had some advice," she whispered, hating how helpless she felt.

Josh turned back to the sink. He stopped moving and rested his hands on the edge of the sink. She couldn't quite tell, but he seemed to be staring at the drain.

It felt like he was drawing away from her, and she didn't

want to overstay her welcome. He'd come to her for advice, but she hadn't been able to give him any. It was probably best if she just left. "Thanks for the drink," she said as she turned to make her way over to the door.

Suddenly, a hand wrapped around hers and she was pulled back to face Josh. He stared down at her as he brought his hand up to her cheek and brushed his fingers against it.

"Beth," he said, his voice low and throaty.

Beth swallowed as she studied him. He was staring at her in an open and raw way. Like he was trying to figure her out, just like she'd been trying to understand him.

"I didn't invite you over here just for chocolate milk."

She took in a shaky breath. "You didn't?"

He shook his head as he leaned in closer. He was inches away from her lips. The intense desire to press her lips to his filled her mind. All she could do was stare at them.

"I like having you around," he whispered as he moved closer.

Beth's hands found their way to his arms and then slowly moved to his shoulders. "You do?"

He nodded as he flicked his gaze to hers. "Yes. You bring me comfort." Then he closed the gap between them as he pressed his lips to hers.

Warmth spread across her whole body as Beth sank into the kiss. It was gentle at first, as if he were asking permission. When she wrapped her fingers around his neck and deepened the kiss, he pulled her to him, pressing her body against his.

Every point of contact seemed to ignite with heat as she melted into him. For a moment, she wasn't sure where he ended and she began. He grabbed her waist and pulled her up onto the counter. Beth couldn't help but giggle.

When they finally came up for air, Beth's lips felt puffy and her eyelids heavy. She felt outside of her body. Her mind was trying to convince her that this had been a dream. That any minute, she was going to wake up and discover that Josh wasn't really here.

But, from her body's reaction to his touch, she knew she was very much awake.

Josh rested his forehead on hers. "That was...unexpected," he breathed as he brought his gaze up to meet hers.

She chewed her lip and nodded. "Yeah."

He pulled back and studied her. Then he reached up and tucked her hair behind her ear. She couldn't help but smile at him.

"Thanks," he said.

Beth furrowed her brow. He kept thanking her. "For what?"

He shrugged as he dropped his hand and grabbed hers. "For helping me when I needed it most. For being here." He smiled up at her, melting her insides. "I was an idiot growing up."

Beth chuckled as she brought up his hand in hers.

"Yeah, you kind of were," she said as she pressed her lips to his knuckles.

He was studying her when she brought their hands back down. His gaze was intense and took her breath away. Not needing to speak anymore, he reached out and pulled her toward him, pressing his lips to hers.

This time, the heat and tension took her breath away. Kissing Zander had never felt like this. It was as if she was made to kiss Josh.

Beth didn't know how long they remained there, kissing. It wasn't until her phone rang that she pulled herself away. Josh was watching her as she shifted to pull her phone from her back pocket. When she glanced down and saw Sam's number, reality came crashing down around her.

What was she doing? There was no way she could have a real relationship with Josh while keeping her mom's cancer a secret. Feelings of selfishness crept up inside of her, which she struggled to push down.

Sure, it wasn't fair that her mom was asking her to keep a secret, but she was the one who was struggling, and she deserved that respect from her family. Right now, her mom's wants trumped her own.

Instead of meeting Josh's waiting gaze, she turned the ringer off. Then she jumped down from the counter. "I should really go," she said, keeping her gaze on the ground. There was no way she could look him in the eye. Then her resolve would fly right out the window.

The fewer people she hurt, the better.

"Beth?" Josh asked, his fingers brushing hers as if asking her to stop.

Gathering her strength, she glanced up at him and forced a smile. "I'll see you tomorrow."

She tried to ignore how confused he looked with his eyebrows pressed together. She wanted to tell him that this had nothing to do with his kiss or how he made her feel. But all of those excuses would lead to questions, and she didn't want to lie to him, but the truth wasn't hers to tell.

Instead, she smiled and turned, grabbing her shoes and leaving without putting them on. Once she was outside and the door was shut, she leaned against the wall of the garage and took a deep breath.

She was in trouble. Oh, she was in so much trouble.

FIFTEEN

THANKFULLY, the next day was Saturday. So Josh could spend the whole day with Jordan, who seemed to be back to his regular, bouncing off the walls self.

It helped to have Jordan be so active today. Josh needed the distraction his son gave him. Especially when his thoughts kept returning to Beth and the mind-blowing kiss they shared yesterday—only to have her sprint out of his apartment faster than a jackrabbit.

He was going out of his mind trying to figure out what he had done wrong, so having to correct Jordan every few minutes was helping him keep his confusion in check.

He was pouring Jordan a bowl of cereal when Sondra burst through the door.

"Josh, thank goodness you are here," she said, clutching her chest like she was having a heart attack.

Josh studied his mom as he poured the milk into the bowl. "Hey, Ma."

She waved away his pleasantry. "No time for that. I need your help."

Josh finished pouring milk in his cereal and brought the bowl up so he could eat without spilling. "What's up?" he asked.

"I'm supposed to sell jams at the festival today, but your grandfather needs me. He fell again, and they are taking him in to get an X-ray, and you know how he gets when he's forced to sit still." Sondra's face fell as stress emanated from her.

A surge of protection rushed through Josh as he nodded. He hated seeing his mom stressed out. "Yeah, sure. What do you need me to do?"

Relief flooded her face. "Everything's packed up in the back of the truck. You need to be there by eight to set up."

Josh's gaze flicked over to the clock. "Ma, it's eight thirty."

Sondra nodded. "I know. You're late."

Josh shoved a few more bites of cereal into his mouth and then set his bowl next to the sink. "Come on, buddy. I need you to move faster." He walked over to his mom and pulled her into a hug and kissed her on the top of her head. "Go. We'll take care of it."

He wasn't sure how much help Jordan was going to be. In fact, he wasn't sure how he was going to run the booth and watch Jordan at the same time.

Which got him thinking...

Reaching into his back pocket, he pulled out his phone. Sondra waved goodbye as she hurried out the door. Josh muttered a goodbye as he brought the phone to his cheek and waited.

"Hello?" Beth's groggy voice filled the air.

Josh couldn't help but smile. Sure, things had been left up in the air last night, but just hearing her voice sent his heart beating faster. "Are you busy today?"

He tried not to get discouraged by the hesitation when she responded, "Not really."

"Good, I need your help. Think you could come by the festival today?"

There was a pause. Josh swallowed, trying to figure out how things could have changed so quickly between them. Last night, there had been a connection. She had to have felt it. He wasn't crazy. He was pretty sure most of Honey Grove had felt it.

"Is it to watch Jordan?"

He wanted to ask if it mattered, but he didn't. "Yes. My mom has to go up to help my grandpa. He fell and is in need of X-rays." He was trying not to read into the fact that he had to have a reason for Beth to come with them. Why didn't she just want to come? Did she not want to spend time with him?

"Oh, I'm so sorry." She grew quiet, and Josh thought she was finished until she said, "Which hospital is he going to?"

He furrowed his brow. "Um, I'm not sure. I think it's St. Jude's."

More silence. "Oh. Okay."

Josh cleared his throat. Why was she being so cryptic? And why did it matter which hospital his grandpa was going to? "So, do you think you could help a guy out?"

"Yeah. I think I can."

Josh decided to push the confusing and awkward parts of their conversation from his mind and focus on the fact he was going to spend his Saturday with Beth. She wasn't going to be his nanny today, but his friend, and deep down he hoped, something more.

JOSH BACKED the truck up to the booth and turned the engine off. Jordan whooped and climbed out of the truck before Josh could stop him.

After pulling the keys from the ignition, he shoved them into his pocket and climbed out of the cab.

"Joshua Braxton?" a small, frail voice said from behind him.

Josh turned to see Mrs. Carey, his elementary school teacher standing behind him. Her white hair was pulled up into a bun, and she was wearing a floral dress.

"Mrs. Carey?" he asked. "It's good to see you." He leaned down and hugged her.

"You, too. My, have you gotten tall." She laughed as he pulled back. "Or I'm just getting shorter."

Josh smiled at her. "Maybe a bit of both?"

She nodded. "Probably." Then she furrowed her brow. "Helping your mom out?"

Josh walked over to the tailgate and let it down. "Yep. Mom had to leave town to help my grandpa, so you've got me."

Mrs. Carey lifted up the crochet purse she was clutching in her hand. "I'm selling next to you," she said, waving to the booth on the other side of the truck.

Josh followed her gesture and then turned to give her a big smile. "That's amazing. Well, we'll have to catch up."

Jordan returned before Mrs. Carey could respond, drawing Josh's attention over to him as he bounced up and down.

"Can I get some quarters to ride the rides?" Jordan asked.

Josh glanced up to see the huge Ferris wheel on the other side of the fair grounds. "Not right now, bud. I need to unpack." He grabbed a box and tugged it closer. It felt light enough for Jordan. "Think you can help me?"

Jordan groaned but then nodded, taking the box from Josh.

Ten minutes later, Josh was sweaty, but the truck was almost completely unloaded. Josh heaved the last box out of the back—who knew that jars of jam weighed this much—and turned, almost running into Beth.

Josh's heart instantly took off as his gaze met hers. "Hey," he said, not stopping the smile that formed on his lips.

Beth cleared her throat as she tucked some hair behind her ear. "Hey. Sorry I'm late. I, um, had to get ready."

Josh let his gaze drop down to her white summer dress and yellow sandals. She looked beautiful.

She shifted under his gaze, and, feeling sheepish, he glanced back up at her. "You look amazing," he said, giving her a wide smile.

Why was she acting so standoffish? Worry filled his gut, and he was trying as hard as he could to muscle it down.

"Thanks." Then she nodded toward the truck. "Can I help?"

Josh heaved the last box onto his shoulder and slammed the gate. "This is it. But I could use your help unloading the jars. Mom always has them all organized nicely. I just don't have the eye."

Beth chuckled, and the sound washed over Josh, making him feel warm. He loved the sound of her laugh.

"I think I can do that."

Jordan was sitting on the ground between the tables of the booth, watching a show. As soon as Beth said hi, Jordan was up and wrapping his arms around her waist.

"Watch out for this one. He may seem sweet, but in about two seconds, he'll be begging for money," Josh said, nodding toward Jordan.

Right on cue, Jordan held out his hand and asked for Beth to take him to the rides.

"Let's help your dad set up, and then we can go," Beth said, tousling his hair.

Jordan didn't seem happy, but he agreed. A few minutes later, they were working side by side, pulling the jars from the boxes and stacking them in intricate patterns. Josh couldn't help but stand back and watch the way Beth was patient and kind with his son.

Jordan would stack the jars, and, even though they were off center or in a blob, Beth would cheer him on, praising his work. It'd been a long time since Josh had seen Jordan beam like that.

When they were finished, Jordan grabbed Beth's hand and demanded that she come with him. Beth met Josh's gaze and raised her eyebrows. As much as Josh wanted to say that she had to stay with him, he nodded.

"You can go. I'll man the booth," Josh said.

Beth gave him a small smile, and for the first time today, it didn't feel forced. It was genuine and felt like the Beth that he remembered. Perhaps her pulling away had all been in his head.

While they were gone, Josh filled the time chatting with Honey Grove residents that stopped to either buy some jam or just shoot the breeze. Apparently, a lot of people had heard he was back, and they all wanted to welcome him home.

He didn't notice how much time had passed until his

stomach growled mid-sentence when he was talking with Mr. Phelps, his baseball coach from high school.

"Sounds like you're hungry, son," Mr. Phelps said, clapping Josh on the shoulder.

Josh rubbed his stomach. "Yeah. I guess so."

"Well, I'll let you get back to it. Make sure to check out the funnel cakes. They are the best," Mr. Phelps said as he waved to Josh and walked to the next booth.

Luckily, a few minutes later, Beth returned with a very tired looking Jordan. He had pink cheeks and his hair was standing up on end from sweat.

"Whoa," Josh said, nodding toward Jordan.

"He needs a little break," Beth said as she exhaled and dropped onto the lawn chair Josh had set up.

Josh grinned. "He's like the Energizer bunny. He just keeps going. And when he's done, it's like full brakes."

Beth laughed as she nodded. Jordan had settled down on a pile of blankets that Josh had gotten from the back of the car. His head was resting on his arm, and his breathing turned heavy.

"Plus, he's had a long day," Josh said, trying to sigh. The truth was they had both had a long day.

Just as he finished speaking, his dad's deep voice spoke up.

"You two look like you could use a break," Jimmy said, clapping Josh on the shoulder and causing him to jump.

Josh's dad stood behind him, wearing a baseball cap and a weary expression. Josh turned and gave his dad a hug.

"You don't mind?" Josh asked, pulling away.

Jimmy shook his head. "Your mom's away. It ain't like I've got anything better to do." Jimmy shoved his hands into his front pockets.

"I'm starving," Josh said, glancing over at Beth, who was studying her phone. Her previous carefree expression had turned serious. He wanted to ask her what that was about, but decided against it. From the look on her face, it didn't seem like she wanted to talk about it.

Food seemed like the best buffer. "What about you, Beth? Some of Mama Chile's Mexican?"

Beth was staring off into the distance, and it wasn't until Josh got closer that she snapped her gaze up to him. "What?" Her cheeks turned red as she flipped her phone over and slipped it into her purse. Then she glanced around. "Food?"

Josh nodded, not sure how to take her reaction. "Yeah. Mexican?"

Beth took a deep breath, and he could see the hesitation in her gaze.

"I mean, if you want to. But don't feel like you have to." He held up his hands and took a step back. It felt like an act of self-preservation, distancing himself from Beth.

"Um..." Beth stared at the ground before bringing her gaze back up. "I guess I can."

Wow. Those weren't the kind of words a guy who was rapidly falling for a girl wanted to hear. He wanted to mean something to her. He wanted her to feel more for him than she'd feel for her boss. Was that ridiculous?

But, she *was* coming with him, so he wasn't going to give her a reason to change her mind. He extended his hand to guide her over to Mama Chile's booth. It took a few minutes to walk there. Beth remained quiet as she stayed in step with Josh.

Josh wished he could read her thoughts. He wished she would just tell him what was going on. There had to be something. She was a normally cheery person. This was not the Beth he knew and cared about.

When they got to Mama Chile's, they ordered and took their order number over to a recently vacated table to sit down. Beth rested her hands on the table in front of her and kept her gaze trained on them. Josh tried a few times to catch her attention, but it was in vain.

Finally, taking a chance, he reached out and wrapped his hands around hers. "Hey," he said, softly.

She jumped as if he'd just shocked her and whipped her gaze up to meet his. He couldn't tell if she was upset or just startled by his sudden touch. Worried he'd overstepped, he patted her hands and then pulled back, wishing that he could take back his blunder.

Her cheeks flushed as she tucked some hair behind her ear. She looked up and gave him a weak smile. "Sorry," she whispered.

If Josh didn't know better, he'd swear he saw tears in her eyes. His heart surged with the desire to protect her.

Whoever was hurting Beth was going to have to answer to him. "What's wrong?" he asked, leaning forward.

Beth shook her head as a tear slipped down her cheek. "It's, um, nothing. Just exhaustion, I think." She dabbed at her eyes with her fingertips as she refused to meet his gaze.

"Beth, something's wrong. You can tell me."

Beth pinched her lips together as she shook her head. She fiddled with the napkin dispenser next to her. She pulled one out and dabbed her eyes. "It's nothing. I promise you, I'm fine."

The weak sound to her voice and the pained expression in her eyes told him she most certainly was not okay. Why was she lying to him? What could she possibly be hiding?

And then realization hit him. She was in love with someone else. Of course. Why didn't that dawn on him before? Here he was, allowing himself to fall for her, and yet, she was having feelings for someone else. And she couldn't tell him because she'd sensed his feelings and didn't want to hurt him.

Gah. He could be such an idiot sometimes.

In an effort to preserve his heart, he leaned back and forced a relaxed expression. "It's okay," he said. His voice came out low. And as much as he tried not to allow it, his tone sounded just as hurt as he felt.

Beth's eyes widened. "Josh, I don't think—"

"It's okay," he repeated. It was one thing to realize what was going on. It was a whole other thing to have her say the words. Call him crazy, but he wasn't sure he could deal with that. At least, not right now.

He should have known better than to open himself up to someone again. Cindy had taught him that love was a joke. That it would only make him into a fool. And here was the proof. Again.

"I understand," he said, tapping his fingers on the tabletop.

"But—"

"Josh Braxton?" The woman in the window called out his name.

Relived that he had an excuse to stand up, Josh made his way over to the counter to grab their food. They ate in silence, and Josh could feel Beth's eyes on him every so often. Even though he wanted to talk to her, to fight for her, he couldn't. He needed to lick his wounds. The ones from Cindy and, even fresher, the ones from Beth.

Tomorrow, he'd feel different. But today, he needed to wallow in his self-pity. It was the only way he was going to survive.

SIXTEEN

BETH

BETH SAT ACROSS FROM JOSH, trying to figure out what was happening. She wanted to tell him the truth. Tell him that her mother was sick. That her prognosis wasn't looking good. But she couldn't tell him that without spilling the secret that her mother had specifically told her not to share.

And, right now, she'd protect her mother's wishes. It was the least she could do.

But it was breaking her heart to watch Josh struggle with what was happening between them. Even though the fact that Josh thought there was something between them made her stomach lighten. It was like all of her wishes were coming true at once, just at the wrong time. Why was fate cruel like that?

Where was this Josh years ago? When they might have

been able to do something about it. When secrets and her mom's illness didn't plague their relationship?

Beth picked up her quesadilla and took a bite. Even though it tasted amazing, the rock in her stomach was heavy and she wasn't hungry.

"Did you have fun with Jordan?" Josh asked. His voice was flat.

Beth grabbed a napkin and covered her mouth as she nodded. "Yeah. He's quite an adventurous boy." She picked at the brown edges of the tortilla, grateful that Josh still wanted to talk to her. "What have you decided about Cindy?"

Josh cleared his throat and took a long sip of his Coke. Then he set it down on the table and glanced over at her. She could see the pain and frustration in his eyes. Even though she wanted to believe that it was all about Cindy, she knew better. She was the cause of that stormy look in his eyes.

"I don't know. I guess I'll have to talk to my lawyer and see what can be done. I mean, she did give up visitation rights."

Beth nodded. She understood where he was coming from, but she also knew what it was like to live in a world where her mother could leave at any moment. No matter what her mother did to her, she'd want the chance to see her. And she couldn't help but think that Jordan might want that chance as well.

"People can change," she said, keeping her voice a whisper. It was something she had to believe because she was here, hoping it would happen between her and her mother.

Josh scoffed as he took a big bite of his taco. "Yeah, but most don't."

Beth kept her gaze focused on her food. "You don't believe that," she said.

When Josh didn't respond, she glanced up to see him staring at her. His jaw muscles were moving as he studied her.

"You think I should let someone who's hurt me back into my life?"

Beth sat up a little straighter. "Yes. People deserve second chances." Things could always be different a second time around.

Josh snorted, which confused Beth. Why was he acting like this?

"Beth, some people don't deserve the second chances we feel we have to give them." He studied her, his gaze intense as he held her own.

This was strange. Did he know? "Well, I choose to live in a world where that isn't the case."

Josh grabbed a napkin, dabbed his lips, and threw it onto his plate as he glanced around. "Well, that's where we differ. I can't let Cindy hurt me or Jordan again. I have his best interests at heart. Cindy? She only wants what's best for Cindy."

Josh's words stung. Sure, Cindy was a horrible person, but that didn't mean she couldn't change, because if that was the truth, then neither could her mom. But her mom *was* changing. Well, partially.

"I'm sorry you feel that way, Josh. It's disappointing that some people can't put past hurts aside and think about the bigger picture." Beth grabbed her plate. After dumping it into the garbage, she glanced over to see Josh staring at her. His jaw was set and his arms folded, and she could tell he was mulling over what she'd just said.

She nodded to him and turned, heading back toward the booth. Even though every ounce of her wanted to run back to her car and drive home, where she'd hide out under her blankets, she couldn't do that. Not when she'd given her word to help Josh. Plus, Jordan would be disappointed if she left.

When she got back to the booth, she found Jordan asleep on the blankets. Mr. Braxton was talking to Jonathan, Josh's younger brother who had graduated with her. They'd been friends that ran in different crowds.

When Jonathan turned, his eyes widened. "Bethy?"

Beth groaned. Great. Why couldn't that nickname have just died? Forcing a smile, she reached out and hugged him. He was no longer the lanky sixteen-year-old who was forced to take her to the prom, but a tall, and ripped, NFL player.

"Jeez, Jonathan," she said, pulling away and squeezing his biceps. "You're making us all look bad."

Jonathan laughed. "Well, I kind of have to be like this. Helps protect me against those linebackers." He winked at her. Last year, he was traded to the Steelers. Beth had tried to see him a few times while she lived in Pittsburgh, but he'd been so busy with the team, and she'd been busy with Zander, it never worked out.

Mr. Braxton announced that he was going to go get one of the funnel cakes that everyone was talking about. Just as Mr. Braxton walked off, Tiffany walked up.

"Beth. I'm happy you came," Tiffany said as she handed off the two snow cones she had in her hands to Jonathan and wrapped Beth into a hug. When she pulled back, Beth made a point to give her a look, hoping Tiffany would understand. She needed her to not mention her mother or the cancer.

Tiffany gave her a supportive smile which helped ease her concerns. She turned to greet Jonathan when she saw Josh walk into the booth and head over to the cab of the truck. Just before he disappeared inside, he met her gaze for a moment. Beth's stomach surged as all of the things she'd said to him—or didn't say to him—rushed through her.

He was hurting, and she was the cause of that pain. But what he didn't realize was she understood him more than he could imagine. She knew what it was like to have a less than ideal parent. But she also knew what it was like to be a child without their parent in their life. It was miserable and lonely.

"Wow, Josh is brooding today," Jonathan said as he took a big bite of the blue snow cone.

"Hey, now, blue is mine," Tiffany said as she grabbed the cone from him.

Jonathan pulled it up, just out of her reach. She dropped

her jaw and gave him a punch. It barely registered on Jonathan's face. Finally, Tiffany gave up, and Jonathan handed it over to her.

Beth wrapped her arms around her stomach as she tried to keep her gaze from making its way over to the cab. Over to where Josh sat. Hurting.

"Hey, what's going on?" Tiffany asked as she tapped Beth's shoe with her own.

Not wanting to get into any of the things plaguing her mind, Beth just shrugged and forced a smile. "Just tired I guess."

Tiffany's eyes widened. "You can't be tired already. Not when we have a night of dancing ahead of us." She raised an arm and wrapped the other one around her waist as she did the cha-cha.

Beth shook her head. There was no way she wanted to stay for the concert that happened at the end of every festival. She wasn't in the mood to dance, and she certainly wasn't in the mood to watch Josh dance.

"I should probably get home. I mean, Mom's coming home—" Just as the words left her lips, regret filled Beth's mind. She needed to get out of here before she spilled everything.

Tiffany was staring at her as she took a bite of her snow cone. Her eyebrows were raised, and Beth knew she'd heard.

"Your mom's not back home?" Tiffany asked, stepping closer to Beth.

"Where'd your mom go?" Jonathan asked.

Beth shook her head. "No. Well, actually, she went over to Jordan to do some shopping. I should probably get back." She hated how there were always so many questions, and she was having a hard time keeping her lies straight.

Tiffany eyed her as she stood in front of Beth.

Hoping that her smile would ward off any more questions, Beth took a deep breath and said, "But I guess it's probably silly, me needing to be there when she gets home." Beth shrugged. "So I guess I'll stay. I can stay."

Tiffany eyed her, and then a smile crept across her lips. "Great."

Beth nodded, and when Tiffany turned to talk to Jonathan, she let her shoulders relax. Well, it looked like she was staying, even if she didn't want to. But, if it kept people from guessing the real reason she wanted to be home, she was doing what her mom asked. And she was going to keep her promise.

IT WAS hard to pretend while everyone around her seemed to actually be happy. Tiffany and Jonathan tagged along with her and Jordan as they went around and played games, once he woke up. Everyone else seemed to be moving around without a care in the world.

Beth, on the other hand, was miserable. Josh refused to look at her when he got out of the cab of his truck. Tricia showed up and went into full flirty mode with him. Josh didn't seem thrilled about it, but he also wasn't pushing her away. The memory of the hospital kept rushing back to Beth, confusing the heck out of her.

By evening, Beth had a headache. She wanted to go home and crawl under the blankets and hide from the world. But, with the way Tiffany was tugging on her arm, she knew she wasn't going anywhere.

The middle of the fair had been cleared to make a large open space. A stage was set up on the far end of the circle, where a band was just starting to tune their instruments.

Tiffany had found a few other people to talk to, so Beth took the time to fade into the crowd. She kept a short distance away from Tiffany, grateful that no one seemed to have a burning desire to talk to her. Once the music started up, everyone cheered and made their way to the center.

Tiffany grabbed Beth's hand and dragged her with. Not wanting to fight her best friend, Beth followed. She tried to act like she was fine, dancing in the crowd, but she wasn't. Eventually, she leaned forward and told Tiffany she needed a drink.

Tiffany nodded, but kept her gaze on a tall, blond that Beth didn't recognize.

Grateful for the escape, Beth slipped through the crowd and over to the table of water pitchers. The evening heat surrounded her, making her more thirsty than ever. After locating a cup, she poured the cool liquid into it. Once she was done, she brought it to her lips and reveled in the feeling of the water as it slid down her throat.

After drinking two glasses, she held the cup in her hand as she glanced around. People on the outskirts of the dance floor were moving slowly to the music as they chatted.

For some reason, being just an observer calmed Beth. She enjoyed just watching instead of forcing conversation when she wasn't in the mood. And lately, that had been happening a lot. It was hard to smile and fake happiness when her life felt like it was crumbling down around her.

"Having a good time?"

Tricia's voice pulled Beth from her thoughts. She turned to see Tricia standing about a foot away with a glass of beer in her hand. Not sure what to say, Beth just nodded. "Yeah."

Tricia took a sip of her drink and then glanced over at her. "I'm surprised you're not out there with Josh." Tricia motioned toward the throng of dancers.

Beth followed her gesture as the mention of Josh's name caused butterflies to flutter in her stomach. "Why are you surprised?"

Tricia shrugged. "Nothing really. Just that I've seen the way he looks at you. I mean, you two have something going on, right?"

Beth swallowed. It felt so right and so wrong to hear Tricia say that about her and Josh. Beth knew she should correct Tricia. Tell her that they were strictly friends and all she did was nanny for him, but she knew that was a lie. Besides, what would Tricia do with that information?

Would she finally make her move on him?

Gah, why did Beth care? She shouldn't. Josh should be

allowed to date whoever he wanted to. He was single, and Tricia was single. They both were looking for someone, and Beth was the last person Josh should fall for. If she cared about him, she'd let him be happy, even if that meant he was happy with Tricia.

"We're not dating. There's nothing going on there." Beth raised her gaze, hoping that she looked stronger than she felt.

Tricia's eyebrows rose. "Nothing. You and Josh aren't seeing each other?"

Beth nodded. "Right. There's nothing going on, and there will never be. I don't think of him like that." Except she did. Every minute of every day. But she just got her mom back, and she wasn't going to blow it again. If Josh was in her life, then her secrets were no longer hers.

Tricia's smile widened as her gaze flicked behind Beth. "Josh, there you are. I've been looking for you everywhere."

Beth's body went numb as she slowly turned to see Josh standing a few feet off. His jaw was set and his gaze hardened as he stared at Beth. Beth's lips parted as every excuse for what she'd said flooded her mind. She needed to tell him that she didn't mean it. That she didn't mean to hurt him.

Anything to wipe that betrayed look from his face.

Right on cue, a slow song blared from the speakers. Beth watched as Tricia walked up to Josh and wrapped her arm around him. Just when she thought she was going to have to stand there and watch them parade around the dance floor,

Josh stepped forward, breaking Tricia's hold, and grabbed Beth's hand.

"We need to dance," he said, leaving Tricia with her mouth open and her protest lingering in the air behind them.

Not sure what to do, Beth followed after Josh as he led her to the dance floor. Before she could protest, Josh wrapped his arm around her back and pulled her close to him. He raised her hand and began leading her around the dance floor.

"We aren't going to leave until you tell me the truth," he said, glancing down at her.

Too startled to speak, Beth just nodded as she followed his lead. As much as she wanted to pull away, she couldn't. The desire to be held by him was quickly taking over her desire to run. And, right now, she was too tired to fight.

She just had to be strong for the duration of a song. She could do that, right?

SEVENTEEN

JOSH

THE FEELING of Beth in his arms as he led her around the dance floor was almost more than he could handle. He was an idiot to grab the girl who had just said there was nothing going on between them. He was the idiot who thought being close to one another might change her mind.

Why did he think that he could change her mind? The length of a song wouldn't be enough to get her to take back the words she'd said about him. What did he think would happen? That she would just confess her feelings for him?

"Was it true?" Exhausted from ruminating, he decided to just speak. If he needed answers, he wasn't going to find them in his own head.

Beth glanced up at him for a moment and then back down to the ground. "Was what true?"

"Don't play with me, Beth. I heard what you said to Tricia."

When Beth didn't respond, Josh braved heartache and tried to meet her gaze, but she wasn't looking at him. Instead, she was staring at his chest as if his shirt held the answers to his questions.

"Well?"

"What do you want me to say?"

Josh dipped down, hoping to catch her gaze. To see if what she said was, in fact, how she felt. "The truth."

Beth's gaze flicked over to his, and he could see the hesitation there. For a moment, he let a flicker of hope burn in his chest that she just might admit how she really felt.

"The truth?" she repeated. From the breathy and hesitant way she spoke, he could tell she was saying it more for herself than for him.

Josh remained quiet, waiting to hear what she would say. Would she tell him? Was their relationship more important than whatever secret she was keeping hidden?

Her gaze rose up to meet his, and he held onto the hope that she would be honest. That he hadn't been a fool to think there might be something between them.

"Josh, I can't." The pain that coated her words caused his stomach to squeeze. She was hurting and he hated that. All he wanted to do was take away whatever was bothering her—if only she'd let him.

"But, Beth, I—"

Beth shook her head. "Please. Don't. I can't..." Tears brimmed on her eyelids as she slowly stopped moving.

All Josh could do was stare at her. Why was she pulling away?

"I should go," she whispered as she dropped her hands and took a step back.

It was like watching a movie in slow motion. No matter what Josh did or said, Beth was leaving. She was walking away from him, and it hurt more than he could say.

He wanted to reach out and stop her. He wanted to tell her that no matter what was going on, they could get through it together. That her pain could be his pain. He wanted her to know that he was here, if she would just reach out and take hold.

But, no matter how long he kept his hand raised, Beth didn't come back. Instead, she gave him a small, weak smile and then turned and left. The crowd swallowed her up. And she was gone.

Rejected and deflated, Josh didn't feel like dancing anymore. Right now, he just wanted to be with his son.

As he passed by the refreshment table, he heard Tricia's high-pitched voice. He tried not to wince as he attempted to evade her. But she was like a bloodhound honing in on his scent.

Just before he disappeared through the booths, her hand closed on his arm, halting him.

"Hey, where are you disappearing too?" she asked as she stepped closer to him.

Josh fought the urge to break her hold and go find Jordan. But, not wanting to be rude, he turned to face

Tricia. She was staring up at him with a hopeful look in her eyes.

And then he felt bad. She was just being nice, and here he was, being a jerk. She was open and honest—something that Beth wasn't. And yet, he was blowing her off.

Taking a deep breath, he turned and smiled at her. It took some focus, but he was able to muscle down the pain that he felt from Beth's abrupt departure.

"Sorry," he said, clearing his throat. "I...I'm just tired." He gave her a weak smile.

It was almost as if Tricia suddenly realized that he wasn't going to hightail it out of there. Her eyebrows raised and her eyes were wide. A giggle escaped her lips as she wrapped her hands around his arm and drew closer to him.

"Well, let's see if there's anything I can do to help you."

Even though there was a pit the size of Texas in his stomach, Josh forced his feet to follow after Tricia as she led him to the makeshift bar near the refreshment table. He even allowed her to order him a drink as he sat on the barstool next to her.

It took two beers for his nerves to calm down and another one before his desire to run after Beth subsided. Thankfully, Sondra stopped by, telling him that they were taking Jordan home, and, from the state he was in, Jonathan should be the designated driver.

Josh just nodded as he kissed Jordan good night and saluted Jonathan.

He spent the rest of the night leaning on the bar as

Tricia talked to him about her house and her divorce. Josh tried to act interested, but every time he let his mind wander, it went straight to Beth.

***

THREE SHARP KNOCKS jolted Josh awake.

He moaned as he covered his face with his hand. Whoever it was could go away. His head felt as if it were splitting in two.

The knocks sounded again.

"Go away," he said, his voice muffled by the pillows he'd buried his face into.

When the knocks came again, Josh growled as he threw off his comforter and stood. "Jordan?" he called out, and then winced as he remembered his mom telling him she'd watch his son for the night. He was alone in the apartment, which was why the person at the door was not giving up.

Not caring about putting on a shirt, Josh shuffled over to the door and unlocked it. He squinted as the early morning light shone through the crack.

Beth.

He blinked a few times, scolding himself for imagining she was standing in front of him. Beth was gone. He even doubted that she'd be his nanny anymore. He'd messed things up royally.

"Well, you look terrible."

Nope. That was Beth. Or someone who sounded just like her.

"Beth?" he rasped. He pinched his lips closed as he swallowed. His mouth felt like death.

"Josh," Beth said. Her voice was soft and caring. And he hated it.

Or he loved it. Right now, his head hurt as much as his heart. "What are you doing here?" he asked, leaving the door open as he walked over to the kitchen sink and filled up a glass of water.

When the latch of the door sounded, fear rushed through Josh. Was Beth still here? Did he want to look?

"I need a favor."

Well, that answered that question. Beth was still here. Great.

Josh took his time draining his glass of water. Then, he wiped his mouth and set the glass down on the counter. Finally, he turned and raised his eyebrows at Beth. "What do you need from me?"

Beth looked irritated but also sad. Frustration boiled up inside of Josh as the need to protect her flooded over him. Why couldn't he just get it through his thick skull that Beth wasn't his to protect?

"I need to borrow your car."

Josh glanced in the direction of her house. "Why?"

"I, um, need to get to Jordan this morning, and my car's battery is dead."

Josh peered back at her. There was something cryptic in

the way she spoke. Like there was more to that story than she was letting on. Was there a guy in Jordan she needed to see? "What's in Jordan?"

Beth hesitated before she cleared her throat and pulled her purse strap higher on her shoulder. "Nothing." She sighed. "I just need to get there."

Well, that wasn't good enough. He wasn't going to let her just walk away from their—whatever they had—to be with this mysterious person in Jordan.

He grabbed his keys off the counter and held them up. "Sure," he said. And as she stepped forward to take them, he slipped them into the front pocket of his jeans. "But I'm coming with you."

Beth's eyebrows shot up. "What? No."

Josh shook his head as he headed toward the bathroom. "Give me five minutes and I'll be ready."

"Josh, you can't come with. Please."

He shook his head as he shut the bathroom door and turned on the shower. He wasn't going to let her off the hook that easy. He was going with her. He was going to see this person that was keeping her from him. And then he'd have words with that person, because as far as he was concerned, he was meant to be with Beth—even if she couldn't see it.

Six minutes later, Josh was showered and dressed. Beth was leaning against the counter, chewing on her thumbnail as Josh walked into the kitchen. She must have not heard him because she didn't turn to acknowledge him when he approached.

Josh took this moment to study her. Her lips were down-turned, and she was staring at the countertop in front of her. Josh could almost feel the stress emanating from her. Something was seriously bothering her, and, for a moment, Josh felt bad about pushing her. Maybe she really didn't want to talk about it. Did it make him a bad friend to push her?

Then he shook his head. No. He wasn't a bad friend. Whatever she was going through, she didn't need to go through it alone. He'd help her. That's what friends do.

"Are you ready?" he asked, allowing himself to reach out and rest his hand on the small of her back. Even though he meant for it to be supportive, he couldn't help but deny the warm feeling that raced up his arm from the contact.

Beth jumped, and Josh pulled his hand away. That had been a mistake. A pained looked crossed her face.

"Josh, I really need to go alone," she said, folding her arms across her chest.

Josh stared at her. "Beth, I..." He wanted to ask her why. He wanted to tell her that he could handle whatever she was trying to keep a secret from him. But would it matter? Probably not.

Beth stepped closer, and, for a moment, he saw the Beth he remembered. The one he felt close to. The one he could tell anything to.

She reached out and held her hand in the air, inches away from him. He wanted to believe that she would touch him. That the kiss they'd shared hadn't only meant something to him.

"Please, let me go alone." She raised her gaze up to meet his.

Josh parted his lips. He wanted to protest. He wanted to beg her to let him go with. That, by going alone, she was shutting the door to him. To them. But, he couldn't do anything to hurt her, and if giving her his keys was the way to bring her happiness, he was going to do it.

So despite the warning bells going off in his mind, Josh reached into his pocket and pulled out his keys. He dropped his gaze as he placed them into her outstretched hand. He allowed his fingers to linger in her palm as he brought his gaze up to meet hers. He wanted her to see just how he felt about her. How he would always feel about her.

The warmth that spread up from their contact exploded in his chest as his heart beat his feelings throughout his whole body. It took all his strength not to reach out and pull her into his arms.

"Here," he said, his voice low and husky. He didn't care. He needed her to know how he felt, even if she wouldn't let him say it out loud.

Beth pinched her lips as she glanced down to his hand and then up to meet his gaze. She studied him. He could see the tears brimming in her eyes. Why was she in so much pain, and why wouldn't she let him fix it?

He held her gaze as he internally begged her to tell him what was wrong. She hesitated and then turned, breaking their contact. He watched as she headed across the living room and out the door before he could get out the words asking her to stay.

Now alone, he swallowed as he rubbed his face with his hands. A feeling of sadness surrounded him, and his shoulders slumped. Even though they technically were never anything more than a nanny and her boss, he couldn't help but feel like this was the end of something.

Something he hadn't realized he needed until it was gone.

EIGHTEEN

JOSH

IT TOOK an hour before Josh felt ready to speak to anyone. After sitting around his apartment, feeling sorry for himself, he finally got up and decided the best thing for him to do was find Jordan and distract himself.

Plus, Jordan deserved a better father than he'd been these last few days. He hated that he'd allowed himself to forget why he was really here. To take care of his son and get his life back in order. And he couldn't do that while mooning away on his couch.

"Hey, guys," Josh called out as he shut the door behind him. He walked into his parents' house and glanced around. No one was here.

"You guys home?" He peered into the living room.

"Josh?" Sondra called from the kitchen.

"Ma?"

"We're in the kitchen."

Josh walked through the living room and into the kitchen. Sondra, Jordan, Jonathan, and Tiffany were sitting at the table. Jordan had a huge stack of pancakes in front of him and was devouring them.

Jonathan and Tiffany were being dished up by Sondra.

"Hey, sweetie. Hungry?"

Josh nodded as he sat down on the chair and held out the plate that had been set. "For your pancakes? You bet."

Sondra laughed as she began stacking pancakes onto his plate. "Great. I've got lots more batter."

When she finished, Josh set his plate back down and drizzled the pancakes with syrup. There was nothing quite like pancakes on a Sunday morning. Josh felt like he was a teenager again.

"Your pancakes can heal the soul, Ma," he said, smiling over at Sondra, who'd made her way back over to the griddle.

Sondra gave him a funny look. "Heal the soul? Why does your soul need to be healed?"

Josh took his time to take a bite and chew. "No reason."

When he glanced over at Tiffany, he saw her studying him. He shot her a funny look, but she didn't look away. It was as if she were trying to figure him out.

"How's the team, Jon?" he asked, glancing over at his brother, who was sopping up the rest of his syrup with his last bite.

Jonathan started in on each player and the assets they brought to the team. Josh enjoyed listening to his brother talk about his passion. It gave him something else to focus on. A great distraction from the gaping hole in his heart.

"Beth's mom has cancer," Tiffany blurted out.

Josh stopped, mid-bite. He glanced over at Tiffany, who had her lips pinched together and her face was crimson red.

"What?" he asked at the same time Sondra came over from around the counter.

Tiffany grabbed her glass of milk and took a sip. Then she set it down and turned her attention back to them. "Joanne has cancer. That's why Beth's been so standoffish."

Josh sat back, feeling as if he'd just been sucker punched. That's why Beth was being so distant? But that didn't make any sense. "I thought she was seeing someone else."

Tiffany snorted like he'd made a joke, but when no one spoke, she glanced around. "Sorry. No. There's no one else."

"No, no, that can't be right. I would know if Joanne was sick," Sondra muttered.

Tiffany shook her head. "Joanne wanted her to keep it a secret. It's been killing Beth." When Tiffany brought her attention back over to Josh, there was a look in her eye that told Josh she'd meant that for him.

"Is that where she's going this morning?" he asked. His mind was going a mile a minute as he tried to figure out what was going on.

Tiffany furrowed her brow and then slowly nodded. "If she needed a ride somewhere, that's probably where she was going. Her mom is in Jordan right now. At St. Jude's."

"St. Jude's? I was just there last night. I didn't see Joanne." Sondra was pacing now. "Poor Joanne. Why didn't she tell anyone?"

Tiffany began pushing her pancakes around on the plate. "I guess she didn't want everyone to feel sorry for her. She made Beth promise not to tell anyone."

"And you know, how?" Josh couldn't help the hurt that crept up inside of him. He'd told Beth about Cindy. About how he was struggling with her wanting to come back into Jordan's life. And yet, she'd hung onto this secret? Like she couldn't trust him?

"It's not like that, Josh. I found out because I looked at her phone. She didn't want me to find out—I'm just nosy I guess."

The urge to get up and move took over Josh, so he stood and began to pace around the kitchen. He took a deep breath as he tried to process what Tiffany had said.

"Can I go watch cartoons?" Jordan asked, completely oblivious to what was going on.

Josh nodded, and before he could say anything else, Jordan was out of the room.

"What are you going to do?" Tiffany's voice broke through his thoughts.

Josh stopped moving as dread filled his chest. What could he do? Beth made it perfectly clear that she wanted nothing to do with him. That she didn't want him to know that her mom was sick. The last thing he wanted to do was force himself into her life when she didn't want him there.

He couldn't deal with that kind of rejection. Not from Beth.

So he let out his breath, his shoulder slumping. "Nothing," he said, and then moved to the back door. He suddenly needed the expansiveness of the outside world.

Just as he shut the door behind him, he heard Tiffany say, "Nothing?"

Now alone, he leaned against the railing and took a deep breath. What was going on? Was this really who he'd become? One of his longtime friends was hurting, and he was just abandoning her?

Because he was worried he'd get hurt?

Man, when did he become such a self-centered jerk.

The door opened behind him, and he shifted when he saw his mom step out onto the stoop. She had a solemn expression on her face as she descended the stairs until she was next to him.

They stood in silence. And even though Josh knew she wanted him to talk first, he was stubborn and waited.

"So, what are you going to do?"

Josh glanced over at his mom. "What are you talking about?"

Sondra gave him her *don't start with me* look. She folded her arms over her apron as she met his gaze. "Don't play dumb with me, child. I know you better than you do. You like that girl."

Josh scoffed as he shook his head. "Ma, don't."

Sondra climbed a step until she was level with him. "Don't what? Tell you the truth? Well, honey, you need it."

Josh rubbed his face. "I can't like her. I just got out of that mess with Cindy. I can't drag Jordan through something like that again. I can't..." His voice drifted off. If he were honest, he couldn't put *himself* through that again. He couldn't let himself reach out to someone who wasn't reaching back.

Sondra folded her arms. "Honey, if we spend our lives thinking about the things we can't do, we'll never have enough gumption to do what we should." Her expression turned serious as she met his gaze head on. "And she's not just some girl you picked up at a bar. You know her. We know her. She's Beth, and that means a whole lot more than some stranger."

Josh studied his mom as her words sunk in. There was some truth to what she was saying. Beth wasn't just some girl. She was...well, she was Beth. And even though ten years had passed since he'd last seen her, that didn't change the fact that he knew her.

He wasn't asking his heart to love someone he barely knew. He was asking his heart to remember the love it felt for someone he'd forgotten he loved.

"But she doesn't want me there." If only his mom knew how Beth had acted this morning when he practically begged her to let him come. When he put his heart out on the line, just to have her reject him.

Sondra gave him a small smile. "She's scared. Her and

her momma have a bad relationship. That's something she's trying to fix. But she can't do it alone. Whatever the outcome of the cancer, Beth needs people there. To support her. Love her." Sondra's expression grew serious as the last two words left her lips.

Josh's heart surged. It was like it was giving him permission to feel that way about someone else again. And if he were honest, all he wanted to do right now was listen to his heart. He was sick of thinking.

"I have to go," he said as he climbed the steps two at a time. Sondra was right behind him, cheering as he pulled open the back door. "I need to borrow your car," he said.

Sondra nodded and pulled the keys down from the pegs next to the door. "I'll watch Jordan for you. You go get her."

"Where are you going?" Tiffany asked, peering around the corner.

Josh gave her a big smile. "To talk to Beth. I have to tell her that I love her. That I'm there for her even if right now she doesn't want me there. I can't leave anything on the table. She needs to know."

Tiffany's jaw dropped as she nodded. "Well...good."

Josh strode over to Jordan and plopped a kiss on his son's head. "I'll be back later, bud. Mind Nana."

Jordan just grunted in response as he shifted to see past Josh. That was the only acknowledgement he was going to get from his son, so he blew a kiss to his mom, patted Jonathan on the back and headed out the front door.

It wasn't until he was inside the car with the engine

running that he realized what he was doing. He took a deep breath as he grasped the steering wheel and said a little prayer. In a matter of moments he was going to lay his feelings out at Beth's feet. He just hoped that it wasn't going to be the major mistake he feared it was.

NINETEEN

BETH

BETH HELD her breath as she rode the elevator to the third floor of St. Jude's hospital. Her heart was pounding in her chest as she shifted her weight. Her nerves were on edge right now. The hour-long drive to Jordan didn't help her anxiety. What did her mother want to tell her?

The text message she got earlier that morning hadn't been very specific. Just that the doctors found something and thought it best to have as much family around as possible.

It couldn't be good if they were calling in the cavalry—the people who loved and cared about her mom to help her get through this hard time.

The elevator dinged and Beth stepped out onto the floor. A nurse's desk sat right in front of her with a few nurses milling around. They were either reading charts or whispering to each other.

Taking a deep breath, Beth stepped up to them. It took a minute for the nurse on the phone to finish and give her a smile.

"How can I help you, sweetie," she said in her southern drawl.

"I'm here to see Joanne Johnson. I'm her daughter." Beth tried to mimic the nurse's smile, but from the way she was feeling right now, she was pretty sure that it came out more strained than relaxed.

The nurse clicked on the keyboard for a moment before turning back to Beth. "She's in room 308. Down that hall, last door on the left," she said, gesturing like a flight attendant.

Beth followed her directions, and, just as she reached door 308, she paused. She needed to take a moment to gather her strength before she walked through the door and found out whatever her mother needed to tell her face to face, instead of over the phone.

It wasn't until this moment that the reality of the situation bore down on her. Her mom was sick. She might never get better. Suddenly, all of the petty fights that she got into as a rebellious teenager seemed ridiculous. How could she have let her relationship with her mother be so affected by them?

If only she'd known that this was her future—her mother's future—she would have made so many different decisions.

"Beth?" Sam's soft voice startled her, causing her to whip around.

Her stepdad was standing behind her with a coffee in his hand. His expression was tired, and she could see the dark rings around his eyes. A surge of emotions rushed through her as she wrapped her arms around her stepdad and just hugged him.

"I'm so sorry," she whispered.

Sam stiffened before he relaxed and patted her on the back with his free arm. "I know," he said.

When she pulled back, Beth had to wipe away a few tears that had escaped down her cheek. She gave Sam a weak smile and then nodded in the direction of the door. "She in there?"

Sam cleared his throat and reached out to turn the door handle. "Yes. And waiting for you."

Beth took a deep breath as she stepped into the darkened room. The drapes had been pulled, but the late morning sun could still be seen shining behind them. As Beth cleared the bathroom, her gaze immediately went to her mom, who was lying on the bed with her eyes closed.

She looked so small and fragile, lying there with the monitors and cords all around her. Her skin was pale and her hair pulled up into a tight bun at the top of her head. Even from where Beth stood, she could see that it was thinning.

Glancing behind her, Beth saw Sam give her an encouraging smile as he lingered in the hall.

Beth nodded, gathering as much courage as she could muster. Blinking back the tears that had formed on her lids, Beth made her way over to the bed and stood a few inches from her mom. She wasn't sure how her mom would feel if she woke her up. But Beth was tired of thinking, so she reached out and slipped her hand into her mom's.

Joanne's eyes fluttered open, and at first, her gaze was hazy. But, after studying Beth's face, a slow smile spread across her lips. "Beth," she whispered.

Stifling a sob, Beth just nodded as she moved to sit on the edge of the bed, still holding her mom's hand. "Hey, Mom," she said.

Joanne's eyes closed for a moment before they opened again. "I'm so happy you came."

Beth stared at her mom. Why would she say that? "Of course I would come."

Joanne's smile softened as she reached over with her other hand. "I'm sorry," she whispered.

Not being able to fight it, a tear slipped down Beth's cheek. "I'm sorry," she said, her voice breaking from the emotions.

Her mom patted her hand a few times. "You are the best daughter a mother could ask for."

Beth pinched her lips together as more tears flowed. She shook her head, hating the way her mother was speaking. It sounded too much like what someone says when they know they're dying.

Her mom lay back on the pillows and took a deep breath. "How are things going with Josh?"

Blinking back her tears, Beth studied her mom. Why was she asking her that? Her heart was breaking for so many reasons today, and she really only had the strength to focus on one at a time.

"It's not going. I broke it off with him." It. What exactly was *it*? They'd kissed, sure, but nothing more. He'd tried to reach out, but she'd kept her distance.

Her mom's expression turned sad. "Why? You've always loved Josh."

Beth swallowed, her emotions lodging themselves in her throat, choking her. "I can't do that anymore. Not when you need me."

Joanne's eyebrows furrowed. "What?"

Was her mom joking? "You need me here. To keep your secret and help take care of you."

A pained expression passed over Joanne's face as she shifted on the bed. "Beth, that is not what I wanted at all." She let out her breath as if moving was akin to running a marathon. "I was just...scared. Secrets are what we use to protect ourselves from the truth." She gave Beth a weary smile. "But don't use them like I do. If you love Josh, tell him."

Beth stared at her mom. "How can I bring him into my life when you want me to keep this a secret?" Beth waved toward her mother's frail body.

Joanne took another deep breath. "Well, that's what I

wanted to talk to you about." She studied Beth for a moment before a smile emerged on her face. "The doctors discovered that the growths are actually shrinking. They are confident that if I have them removed, I could actually beat this thing."

Beth stared at her mom. What? She opened her lips and then shut them again. "You're going to be okay?" Throwing caution to the wind, Beth reached over and wrapped her arms around her mom's small shoulders. This was a hug type of revelation.

Joanne chuckled as she patted Beth's back. "It's not guaranteed, but my chances are looking a lot better now."

Beth pulled back, this time allowing the tears to flow. "This is the best news," she said.

Sam walked into the room with a wide smile. "You told her?" he asked.

Joanne nodded.

Beth glanced over at him, and for the first time in a long time, saw complete joy on his face. She glanced back over to her mom and then back to Sam. It'd been a long time since she'd felt like she belonged. Things weren't perfect and there were still broken things that needed to be fixed, but she felt hopeful.

Her mom had a chance. Which meant their relationship had a chance.

The only thing that would make things perfect would be if she could fix things with Josh. But she'd pretty much ruined that this morning. There was no way he was going to want her as his nanny or anything else. Not after the way she'd treated him.

She spent the afternoon with her mom. They ate lunch and watched ridiculous soap operas on the TV. Beth couldn't help but smile. It was like she was a kid again. The stress that had surrounded them had lightened. It was as if the news about her mom was just what their family needed to heal.

Her recovery still wasn't for sure, but, for the first time in a long time, she felt hopeful.

Joanne's eyes drifted closed, so Beth excused herself. Her mom needed all the rest she could get.

After slipping out into the hall, Beth took the elevator down to the gift shop. She smiled at the stuffed animals that lined the walls. After buying a bag of dark chocolate and a Sprite, she left the shop. She was studying her receipt as she made her way out into the entryway.

"Umph," a deep voice said as she ran straight into someone.

Embarassed, she glanced up to apologize, only to see Josh peering down at her.

Her jaw dropped open as he blinked a few times. He looked as surprised as she was.

Furrowing her brow, she stepped back just in case she was seeing things—there was no way Josh was here. But, no matter how many times she blinked, Josh remained, staring her down.

"What are you doing here?" she finally brought herself

to say when Josh didn't offer an explanation for his sudden appearance.

He cleared his throat and pushed his hands through his hair. "I, um..." He glanced around. "Tiffany told me where to find you."

Realization settled around Beth. Of course. "She did?"

He nodded. And then a pained look crossed his face. "She said something about your mom?"

Right. Beth moved out of the way as a nurse wheeled a man down the hall in a wheelchair. Josh followed her, and she couldn't help the way her stomach lightened at his nearness.

"Yeah. My mom...has cancer," she said, the last part coming out in a whisper. She could feel Josh's stare on her as she swallowed. It was hard to say out loud. She'd kept it quiet for so long, it was like it didn't exist.

"I'm so sorry," Josh said, reaching out and letting his fingers linger closer to her arm.

Goosebumps rose on her skin as if anticipating his touch. But it never came.

Beth let out her breath. "Yeah, but we just got some good news. The tumors are shrinking, which means Mom can get them removed." Beth glanced up and gave him a weary but hopeful smile.

The expression on Josh's face morphed into one of elation. He studied her as he shoved his hands into his pockets. She wanted to believe it was because he wanted to touch her but was stifling that desire. Was it too much to hope?

And then guilt and frustration with herself and the situation she'd put him in rushed over her. She was the one who'd kept her distance. As much as she wanted to believe that walking away from Josh had more to do with her mother's cancer than her own fear of love, she knew that wasn't the whole truth.

Zander had hurt her. Made her believe that she was unlovable.

"Beth..." Josh started as he stepped forward, ending inches away from her.

Already emotionally exhausted, Beth glanced up to meet his gaze. It was warm and inviting. Like he knew everything she was trying to say without actually saying it.

"I'm sorry," she whispered.

As if that was the key to his release, Josh reached up and cradled her cheek in his hand. He held her gaze as he wiped away the tear that had slipped down. "Beth, you and I have both been hurt." He reached up to tuck her hair behind her ear. "But I can't deny how I feel about you anymore. I want you in my life. I need you there. You understand things about me that I don't think anyone else ever will."

He gave her a hopeful smile as he leaned in and pressed his lips to her forehead. "If there is any secret you need me to keep, I'll keep it. Your worries are my worries. Your joys are my joys."

Beth closed her eyes as her heart swelled with love for Josh Braxton. He moved down to press his lips to the tip of her nose. "Let me in, and I promise I will never hurt you." He pulled back to hold her gaze.

Another tear slipped down as she nodded. It felt so good to be honest with Josh. This was what was missing in her life. Love.

It was an amazing feeling. Going from feeling alone to building a relationship with her mother and Josh. It was everything she'd ever wanted.

"Are you sure?" she asked, reaching out her free hand and resting it on his arm.

Josh gently took her purchases from her and set them on the ground. Then he wrapped his arms around her waist and pulled her close.

"Beth Johnson, I can't promise everything will be perfect. I can't promise that we won't fight. But I can promise that I will protect you until the day I die. That your happiness will be the one thing I live to create."

He bent down and pressed his lips to hers for a moment before pulling back. As he stared down at her, Beth's heart pounded so loud that she could hear it in her ears.

"Will you let me?"

A smile spread across her lips as she nodded. Then, lifting up onto her toes, she pressed her lips to his again. This time, more forceful and full of passion and love. Everything that she felt for him, she expressed through that one kiss.

When he finally pulled back, a soft chuckle escaped his lips. "I love you, Beth."

She glanced up at him. "I love you too, Josh."

They held each other's gaze for a moment longer before Josh dipped down and wrapped his arms around her. Not holding back, Beth met his kiss with every emotion welling up inside her.

No matter what the future brought, she knew that with Josh by her side, she could accomplish anything. And she'd live her whole life making sure he felt the same.

EPILOGUE

JONATHAN

JONATHAN WAS SITTING on the couch when Josh came into the living room later that night. He'd been in Jordan all day, supposedly trying to win back the girl he'd fallen in love with.

Which was strange for Jonathan to think about, because to him Beth was still that girl he'd grown up with. The girl he'd run around with as a teenager, raising hell.

But, from the goofy look on Josh's face, Jonathan could tell that his brother didn't share his sentiments.

"Were you successful?" Jonathan asked as he set his phone on the side table.

Josh sighed and collapsed on the chair across from him. He rubbed his thighs with his hands as he leaned back and closed his eyes. "Oh yeah," he said as he tipped his face toward the ceiling.

"Okay, too much," Jonathan said, raising his hand. Sure,

his brother was the date one girl and settle down type of guy, but Jonathan wasn't. Besides, Corinne had broken his heart, and he wasn't sure anything could ever fix it.

Josh glanced over at him. "What's up with you?"

Jonathan shifted on the couch as his brother stared him down. Four years his junior, he'd always looked up to his older brother, but it wasn't until after college that they'd gotten closer. With the way Josh was studying him, he worried that the elephant-sized wound inside of him was visible.

"Nothing," Jonathan said, forcing his signature cocky smile.

Josh furrowed his brow as he straightened and folded his arms. Jonathan could tell his brother didn't believe him, but he didn't push it. Josh glanced around. "Where's Jordan?"

Grateful for a question he could actually answer, he motioned toward the back of the house. "Mom took him outside. Said something about a water balloon fight." Jonathan shrugged.

Josh cleared his throat and stood, stretching in an exaggerated movement. He straightened and walked over to Jonathan, clapping him on the shoulder. "Don't discount love so fast, little brother. You never know who's waiting just around the corner." He gave Jonathan a wink.

Jonathan shook his head. "Yeah, I don't think so. One, I'm way too busy, and two? Who would I date?"

Josh gave him a knowing smile. "Trust me, fate is funny like that. Just when you think you've thrown in the towel on love, people start popping up around you." He rubbed his hand through his hair as he made his way over to the kitchen. "She's just around the corner. 'Cause if it can happen to me, it'll happen to you."

Before Jonathan could retort, Josh was gone.

Now alone, Jonathan returned to the distraction of his phone. He glared at the screen as Josh's words raced through his mind.

What did Josh know anyway? He'd found the perfect girl for him. In Jonathan's world, women like that didn't exist. They either wanted him for his money or his status. It was hard to find a girl who just liked him for him.

His heart squeezed at the thought of finding someone who had the qualities he was looking for. It shouldn't be hard, but with his luck, it felt near impossible.

He shook his head. Just because one Braxton brother found love, didn't mean it was in the cards for him. He was happy for his brother, but he needed to manage his expectations for himself. If he didn't get his hopes up then he couldn't get hurt. And, right now, protecting himself was all that mattered.

Love wasn't going to happen for him. Period.

***

Fall in love with Jonathan and Tiffany in the next Braxton Family Romance,

Friendship Blooms in Honey Grove

HERE!

Jonathan is back home in Honey Grove. He's ready to forget the stresses of his job and the fact that everyone around him is finding love, except him.

Tiffany can't seem to hold onto any relationship. Thankfully, Jonathan is the only constant guy in her life and someone she never has to worry about losing.

Now dateless for her cousin's wedding, it only makes sense to go with someone safe—Jonathan.

A fake relationship between the two of them started out as a way to keep themselves protected...until the feelings between them begin to feel real.
Discover the book, HERE!

***

If you want to connect with Anne-Marie Meyer, join her newsletter and receive Fighting Love with the Cowboy for FREE!

Sign up HERE!

Also join her on these platforms:
Facebook
Instagram
anne-mariemeyer.com

37824294R00135